FACE TO FACE
with Indian Publishing Professionals

FACE TO FACE
with Indian Publishing Professionals

S.K. Ghai

INSTITUTE OF BOOK PUBLISHING

INSTITUTE OF BOOK PUBLISHING
A-59, Okhla Industrial Area, Phase-II, New Delhi-110020.
Tel: 26387070, 26386209; Fax: 91-11-26383788
E-mail: mail@ibpindia.org
www.ibpindia.org

Face to Face with Indian Publishing Professionals
© 2012, Institute of Book Publishing
ISBN 978 81 207 7174 1

All rights are reserved.
No part of this publication may be reproduced, stored in a retrieval system or transmitted, in any form or by any means, mechanical, photocopying, recording or otherwise, without prior written permission of the original publisher.

Printed in India

Printed by Sterling Publishers Pvt. Ltd.,
New Delhi-110020.

Dedicated to

Bauji and Mataji

who taught and encouraged
me to grow in publishing

Foreword

This volume presents 27 interviews conducted with professionals from the publishing industry in India. I have read them over a period of time as they have appeared in the e-journal *Publishing Today*, but it is a delight to have them gathered together in one book.

The professionals provide valuable insights into the industry in India, at a time when new entrants continue to arrive, attracted by the fast-expanding market for books. For example, it has just been announced in February 2012 that Bloomsbury will create a new operation, with the brief to develop Indian authorship and publishing programmes, headed by one of the interviewees in this volume, Rajiv Beri.

Browsing through this book will give the reader a strong impression of the vibrant domestic publishing scene, whilst many of these companies are also operating in international markets. We find here, to give a few examples, information about a 3,500-strong sales team, selling books door to door; the growing shoots of a revolution in digital publishing and web-based learning; and of high-profile literary debuts of Indian authors.

We learn about the personal philosophies of many of the professionals interviewed, as well as about their typical working day. I am sure that this collection will inspire young people wishing to pursue a career in publishing and persuade them to make the most of their working lives. The volume reminds us all of the value of books – as Bipin Shah says (page 33):

'A good book is one which opens a new window of your mind or brings in a fresh breeze of ideas.'

Angus Phillips*

---

*Angus Phillips is Director of the Oxford International Centre for Publishing Studies at Oxford Brookes University. He is the co-author (with Giles Clark) of *Inside Book Publishing* and the Editor-in-Chief of the publishing journal *Logos*.

Foreword

I met Mr S.K. Ghai when he led a trade mission of Indian publishers to New Zealand. Two characteristics immediately strike you about Mr Ghai. The first is his love for life, his good humour, his kindness. He is a joy to be around. The second is his passion for the Indian publishing industry, and for its advancement.

This book is a product of the second characteristic, but clearly has been influenced by the first. To wish to share the experience of so many talented and knowledgeable industry colleagues is laudable. To get them to talk so openly and so informatively is what makes it special, and gives much to Indian publishing.

The entire publishing world has a fascinating, and challenging, few years ahead. You in India have even more opportunities and challenges than the rest of us. Hopefully, many participants, especially newer and younger, in publishing will read this and learn from it. Well done to all of you.

With very best wishes,

Kevin Chapman BBS, MBA (Hons)
President,
Publishers Association of New Zealand

Foreword

Can publishing be defined as a profession at all in India? This is not an out-of-the-box question because it was asked by an eminent Indian librarian at the inaugural meeting of the short-lived Association of Publishing Professionals in India (APPI) in the early 80s and has been repeated time and again in different forums. The librarian rightly said that here was a profession that required no course of formal study as a prerequisite for entry "into this occupation for gentlemen." Probably the librarian had a cricketing metaphor in mind where he made a distinction between 'gentlemen' who described themselves as 'amateurs' because they played for fun while the 'players' were 'professionals' who played for payment!

Whatever the motives of the librarian, the unwritten text implied that professionals were better in the game than the mere amateurs. But there was a great deal of truth in his observation because if you read the biographies of eminent publishers who have left a mark on the book world none had a formal training; they learnt the 'ropes' of publishing through sheer dint of hard work—editing, production, marketing and accounting—on the job. Indeed, Kurt Wolff, a leading German publisher and scholar, puts it across straight:

"There is no training that will make a publisher; but one ought to have taste, literary discrimination and a grand passion for work undertaken, along with the patience of an all-forgiving lover, since by definition, every creative artist is unbalanced."

This isn't an easy qualification to fulfill but is the only one which brings out the best: the stamina for long-distance 'running' in a field where many drop out of the race.

But a working definition of what makes a publishing professional is required if we have to get anywhere. And it would be someone who is in the publishing *business* (the operative word is *business*) who "depends entirely or largely on their employees to carry out and supervise all specifically publishing operations". As the doyen of Indian publishing, the late Samuel Israel put it, 'Publishing operations' are many and complex but 95 percent is commonsense made complicated, and even the remaining 5 percent, the essential reasoning, if not all the technical details (especially when it comes to finance and copyright law), can be explained in plain terms.

As in any other profession, the best way to explain principles is by using them to understand problems that interest the common reader. Surinder Ghai's interviews with leading Indian publishers—they read like a roll call of all who matter in Indian publishing today, both in English and regional languages—in a Q and A format covers the entire gamut of problems faced by Indian publishers who have had a hands-on experience with the business of publishing. This is what gives value to the interviews because they are all based on the lived experience of the interviewees, rather than a systematic text-book approach.

Face to Face with Indian Publishing Professionals is the sequel to his earlier work, *One to One: Glimpses of Indian Publishing Industry*. Surinder's modus operandi to provide an overall view of the Indian publishing scene is straightforward: he interviews each Indian publisher who has contributed to developing a specifically Indian list (as distinct from the colonial heritage of Indian publishing) and evaluates how they started off and the areas they have been identified with, whether educational or general books, and how they went about organising distribution which was, and still is, one of the most difficult tasks of an Indian publisher. (According to Rajen Mehra, who has established Rupa as one of the leading Indian publishers, distribution is the key to the success of Indian publishing because of the difficult terrain in which we have to function as well as the scarcity of distribution outlets outside the main metros.)

For those who are in the know and have migrated from larger publishing houses to set up their own, the value of these interviews lies in the wide array of entrepreneurs who have taken to publishing. Surinder has covered them all, or at least nearly all.

Jason Epstein, a book publishing editor with Random House since 1958 said towards the close of his professional career in 2000 that he "favoured the God Janus, who faces backward and forward at once. Without a vivid link to the past, the present chaos, and the future unreadable." Many who remain critical of the Indian publishing scene should perhaps keep in mind the ground that has been covered since Independence. Surinder Ghai's two books show us some of the road less traveled.

Ravi Vyas
Publishing Professional

Preface

There is a buzz in the Indian publishing industry, Indian authors are participating in national and international literary festivals with full enthusiasm and vigour and receiving high acclaim from the readers. Indian publishers are participating in major international Book Fairs be it London, Frankfurt, Bologna, Gudalajara, Tokyo, Beijing or Nigeria.

Education in India has also spread its wings in each and every part of the country. We have more than 1.20 million schools, 20,000 colleges and 343 Universities. India enjoys a special position, perhaps the only one in the world, where publishing is being done in 24 languages, resulting in an immense growth in regional language publishing and in its distribution network.

The retail space has increased manifold in the last 10 years and will continue to increase rapidly in the coming years due to the arrival of shopping malls in major metros, state capitals, and big and small towns in the country. This has certainly given an impetus to the display of books. With this regional language books have started selling as there is a designated area for local language books in the malls. All these factors have made the Indian book industry a rapidly developing and exuberant industry.

With production standards at par with international standards, and sales of books in English and in regional languages increasing, many multinationals have begin their operations in India. They have started publishing in regional languages as well.

Even though the industry is going through this very healthy and prosperous phase, there exists a vacuum within the industry in sharing information and ideas. Individual publishers are doing a remarkable job and this is the reason why the industry has been getting attention from the media and has been able to release and make bestsellers. What is missing is a common platform for publishing professionals to interact with each other regarding issues concerning them.

Keeping this in mind, in Dec 2006 I started Publishing Today, an e-journal, which serves as a forum for publishing professionals as well as others to share information and exchange views. In every issue I try to include an interview with a publishing professional and news about the industry. Most of the professionals interviewed by me have been very forthcoming in sharing their experiences and this excellent response has kept me going as I have known them for decades.

Having interviewed such distinguished personalities over a period of time, my wish to share their experiences with a wider audience took the shape of a book. A book which would be helpful to budding professionals and new entrants in widening their vision about the industry. The need to compile these inspiring interviews into a book format arose because I felt that their accessibility was limited only to a scattered few and also because many publishers would rather enjoy a printed book than surf online.

I brought out *One to One: Glimpses of Indian Publishing Industry*, containing first fourteen interviews, in March 2008, which was well-received. Since then I have interviewed 27 more publishing personalities, edited in volume II *Face to Face with Indian Publishing Professionals*.

The present book also contains a tribute article on Tekkatte Narayan Shanbagh who passed away in February 2009 and my own interview taken by Prof. G.S. Jolly on being elected as Chairman, on the Books, Publications and Printing panel of CAPEXIL, an export promotion council under Ministry of Commerce and Industry, Government of India.

I am very grateful to all the professionals whom I have interviewed in the years gone by for their wholehearted support in this venture.

I am also grateful to Angus Phillips, Kevin Chapman and Ravi Vyas for writing the foreword to this book at a short notice.

S.K. Ghai
skg@sterlingpublishers.com

25th February, 2012

Contents

	Foreword by Angus Phillips	vii
	Foreword by Kevin Chapman	ix
	Foreword by Ravi Vyas	x
	Preface	xiii
1.	**A S Chowdhury** Work hard and be patient	1
2.	**Arvind Kumar** Practice the Gandhian principle of self-denial	9
3.	**Asoke K Ghosh** Our STM books are accepted all over the world	16
4.	**Balram Sidhwani** A good book gives directions to life and thinking	24
5.	**Bipin Shah** Visibility is equally important as making new contacts	29
6.	**Chiki Sarkar** Create an atmosphere for reading and writing	34
7.	**Dhanesh Jain** Competition is good for growth	40

8. Gandhi Kannadhasan 45
   Website is an investment and not an expense
9. Geeta Dharmarajan 54
   Start day with prayer and end it with prayer
10. J P Vij 61
    No competition in the field of medical publishing
11. Kamal Ahuja 67
    Always remember the best is yet to come
12. M G Arora 73
    Success is not a destination but a journey
13. Nuzhat Hassan 81
    Road to the 'best' is always under construction
14. R K Mehra 85
    Distribution is the key to success
15. Rajiv Beri 90
    Contribute towards the upliftment of education
16. Ritu Menon Padma Shri 96
    A good book endures, the way you think
17. S C Agarwal 101
    Learning has no age
18. S K Ghai 104
    The world is a book and he who stays at home reads only a page
19. Saniyasnain Khan 111
    Writing is the byproduct of reading

20. **Saugata Mukherjee** — 116
    Publisher should be professional and open to change
21. **Shyam Deshpande** — 123
    Publishing is a social responsibility
22. **Sridhar Balan** — 129
    Publishing is a creative profession
23. **Sukumar Das** — 136
    Be good to others, they will be good to you
24. **Sunil Mehta** — 141
    Selling on cash in the best policy
25. **Tekkatte Narayan Shanbhag** — 148
    From a Bookstall owner to a legendry Bookseller
26. **Vikas Gupta** — 153
    Books are the only commodity that is cheaper in India
27. **Vikas Rakheja** — 159
    Transparency and integrity helps in building a brand

Index — 165

Contacts — 173

A S CHOWDHURY

Managing Director
Goodwill Books International and
Chowdhury Export House

Work hard and be patient

At 78, you are still very active in business, travel quite often, enjoy life and keep yourself in a happy mood always. What are the reasons?

I lead a very disciplined life. I exercise daily by walking for about 4 km and have my breakfast at 6 am, irrespective of whether it is a Sunday or a holiday, or whether I am in India or abroad. I am strictly vegetarian and avoid overeating. I believe in doing one's own work as much as possible and not keeping any expectations from anyone whatsoever. At the same time, I am not at all egoistic and try to remain calm.

I learnt that you had a humble start and saw a lot of difficulties in the early years of your life. Share some memories with us.

I started working at the age of 13, when I migrated from Pakistan, by selling fruits and other things on streets, although there was no financial burden on me or my family, but just to keep myself busy before joining the new academic session of the school which was to begin 6 months after I started working. This helped me a lot in developing confidence and ability for doing any type of work.

You shifted from Hotel Janpath to Indian Airlines and then to National Productivity Council (NPC) before actually coming to publishing. Any reasons?

After completing BCom (Hons) and National Diploma in Commerce and Business Administration, I joined as an accountant in Hotel Janpath, selected out of a total of 273 candidates for the job. I shifted to Indian Airlines for better opportunities and better prospects, and again, for the same reasons, to NPC.

What was the motivation to come to publishing?

The aim of my life was to start a restaurant but while I was working at NPC in Bombay in the year 1961, I started compiling a book on jokes which I gave to my uncle Dev Raj Verma of Kiran Publications, and it became a big hit. This gave me the confidence to go ahead with another book on the same subject. When I went to offer the same to my uncle, he offered me the same amount of Rs. 400 for full copyright as he had done for the first book. But I demanded Rs. 1000 which he refused. At this, I decided to publish it on my own and this way I came into the publishing business.

In 1970s, you advertised a lot in the print media. What was the experience like?

I gave full page advertisements in Indian Express, Illustrated Weekly of India and some other papers for launching a new magazine named *Career Events – Passport for Success* for the students appearing in competitive examinations. Despite the best writers, good marketing strategy, and the best of salesmanship, the magazine flopped and I ran into heavy losses.

Which was your first destination when you started exporting books and how did it go?

I started exporting books to Thailand in 1970, which even today is not an English-speaking market, and procured very small orders.

Which export market are you concentrating on and what is your USP?

In my initial years in export, I confined myself mostly to South-East Asian markets, which I am maintaining till today, though we do export to some other countries outside this region also.

You distribute other publishers' books in the export market. Do you experience any hindrances?

We export books of more than 200 publishers and do face a number of difficulties. Sometimes the publishers do not supply enough promotional material or deliver the goods well in time resulting in the delay of supplies and sometimes lose the order altogether.

What are the reasons for the increase in the export of books and how can it increase further?

There is no second opinion that the quality of Indian books is one of the best in the world today and that is the reason why the exports are increasing day by day. It can increase further if publishers and the government implement the following steps:

a) Publishers should provide sufficient promotional material to the exporters;

b) Publishers should undertake foreign visits to promote their books. Their efforts should be complementary rather than competitive;

c) Publishers should improve their bindings; and

d) The government needs to give more subsidies to the exporters in respect of export incentives, MDAs, etc. as the export of books is still not as advanced as in other countries.

Do you think CAPEXIL is performing its role well? What more do you expect from it?

I would like to congratulate Capexil for the excellent co-operation it has been extending to the exporters, particularly in the last 3-4 years, and they can do a little more by trying to participate in as many international book fairs as possible, and helping the exporters by providing MDA as at present the assistance provided is not sufficient in view of the heavy rentals and travelling expenses.

What is your relationship with various Publishing and Booksellers Associations?

I have always been active in almost all the federations and associations associated with the publishing industry which include Federation of Indian Publishers, Federation of Publishers and Booksellers Association of India, Delhi State Booksellers and Publishers Association, and Federation of Educational Publishers and have great respect for all the associations and would always be glad to do every possible thing for publishing and export.

You have been the Election Officer of FPBA a number of times. Why do they always select you and do you enjoy working for it?

Till today I have been Election Officer for 14 times in DSBPA, FPBA and Federation of Educational Publishers, and I am proud to say that on a couple of occasions I was able to persuade the other candidates to withdraw where there was neck to neck competition and all the 14 elections resulted into unanimous decisions.

You have been honoured by various publishing bodies. What all awards have been conferred to you? Which one is the most dear to you?

I have been honoured with the following awards:

1. For Outstanding Contribution to Book Industry from DSBPA 1998
2. For distinguished services from FEPI 1999
3. Jampur Ratan from Jampur Welfare Association 2000
4. Export Promotion Award from FEPI 2000
5. Best Exporter of the Year from DSBPA 2001
6. Certificate of Merit from Capexil 2001-2002
7. Best Exporter Award from FPBA 2002-2003
8. Certificate of Merit from Capexil 2003-2004

9. Life Time Achievement Award from FPBA 2009
10. 50 years in Book Industry Award FPBA 2010

In addition, I have received several awards from charitable associations and the most cherished award is the lifetime achievement award from FPBA and *Jampur Ratan* from Jampur Welfare Association.

How have you divided the work between your sons and yourself?

My younger son, Rajneesh Chowdhury, runs two publishing houses, namely Goodwill Publishing House and Young Learner Publications, and is also a partner with me in Chowdhury Export House and Goodwill Books International. On the other hand, my elder son, Amber Raj Chowdhury, runs two publishing houses – Academic India Publishers and Angel Publishing House – and is involved in the exports as well.

Do you love travelling?

Even now I have to travel for about a week or 10 days in a month. Although these are all business trips, I enjoy every visit irrespective of the fact whether I get business or not since it keeps me fit and disciplined.

What do you like to read?

I do not get much time but I read newspapers and magazines.

What do you think defines a good book?

Every book is a good book just like any film is a good film as long as it gives you something or the other to learn and enjoy and it all depends on the individual how he or she takes it.

What is your message to the young publishing professionals?

They need to work hard and be patient as there are plenty of opportunities in the industry which are not being fully availed by the trade.

What is your message for a happy and healthy life?

In this modern, fast-moving world we all are living under great stress – stress related to business, family, health and so on.

It is impossible to avoid stress completely but we certainly can lessen it to a great extent by observing the following principles:

1. Peace at any price is cheap. Any sacrifice made for it is worth it and one should not feel any humiliation in anyway.
2. Ego and anger are very dangerous for man; they destroy families, they destroy businesses, in fact they destroy everything and result into nothing except tension, pressure and ill-health.
3. Always avoid expectations, particularly, from your own family members – son, daughter, grandchildren or even your husband or wife – because expectations, when not fulfilled, create havoc on your brain leading to hypertension, high blood pressure, diabetes and even heart attack.
4. Try to put your best foot forward in business, family or whatever you do and even if the results are not very positive, you will still be happy because you have done your best.
5. Try to make others happy as much as you can. Your happiness will come automatically because the blessings of those people will be so strong and powerful that the Almighty will be forced to give you all the happiness.
6. Try to donate as much as possible and remember that this is the only credit you will carry with you after you leave this world.
7. Clear all your debts, whether personal or professional, well in time before it is too late in life.

8. Try to help others as much as you can, particularly your maids, servants and drivers, who serve you day and night and are rather closer to you than your own relatives.
9. Always try to be independent, doing as much as you can on your own – this will make things simpler and easier for you.
10. Do not consider yourself too intelligent. Always listen to others patiently before coming to any conclusion.
11. Always remember that man moves towards death the day he is born. This will help you to follow the righteous path.

(Publishing Today, February-March 2012)

ARVIND KUMAR
Consultant
A&A, Arvind Kumar Publisher

Practice the Gandhian principle of self-denial

What made you leave the cushy Scholastic job to start your own?

During my 8-year stint at Scholastic India, I completed the basic task of setting up the company, creating relationships with more than 5000 schools all over the country and refining the model of school book clubs and school book fairs. After accomplishing this, I felt that the company no longer required the leadership of a pioneer and instead could now be managed by professional managers. I decided to move on, though I am still connected with Scholastic Inc., as a business associate but not an employee. In the last couple of years, besides our independent publishing, we have introduced 88 Scholastic titles in Indian languages. We published these against firm orders without building any inventory.

From Auto Engineering in Czechoslovakia to Publishing in India — two professions which are poles apart! Any specific reason for the shift?

My father was a visionary, a great publisher, yet he wanted me to set up a big automobile service center. After completing graduation, I completed a course in auto engineering from Czechoslovakia. However, my mind was in publishing and I wrote to my father about my preference. I spent a few months assembling medimobiles (ambulances) in Germany, and then went to Britain for further studies. I also took up a job for making a living. This helped me to study cost accountancy and management. I also tried my hand at a mail order bookshop before I returned to India in 1968, to join my father's publishing house.

How did you handle Radhakrishna Prakashan and what direction did it get under you?

The canvas was small in the family publishing house. We published literary works, textbooks and children's books in Hindi. We were also a vendor to the Library of Congress Office for Hindi books. Yet, due to the nature of the business, we were largely dependent on the Universities for textbook prescription and government departments for bulk purchases. I was successful, yet not happy with the corruption that was creeping in the textbook prescription as well as the government purchases. Initially, my reaction was to discontinue our dealings with the Universities. After a few years, I found myself at crossroads – I had two choices; either to join the corrupt practices or to fight them. I decided to FIGHT and attacked corruption and the corrupt officials through our house journal, *Samayik Sahitya*, posted every month to eight thousand addresses. While it attracted attention of the media and the government, it also fuelled opposition to me. Despite this, I contested the election for the position of President, Akhil Bharatiya Hindi Prakashak Sangh (All India Association of Hindi Publishers) and got 51% votes (the other two candidates shared the remaining 49%)

How was your journey in publishing till you joined as Director, NBT?

As the President, I served on the National Book Development Council, and when the Council constituted a five-member working group to formulate a National Book Policy, the leaders of the industry recommended my name. Other members of the working group were Kanti Choudhury, K S Duggal, Dr D P Pattanayak and Kala Thairani (member-secretary). We spent a year going around the country, meeting with authors, educationists, intellectuals, librarians, publishers and others with a stake in books and reading. This enhanced my interest in book promotion and I agreed to take up the challenge of directing the National Book Trust, India. Another reason for this shift was to do something positive rather than to continue the bitter campaign against corruption. Nevertheless, my distracters tried blocking my appointment, and I had to wait for 13 months before the cabinet committee for appointments headed by the Prime Minister, approved my name for the position.

I think you were the first Director of NBT who came from publishing but you were not very friendly with publishers at that time. Any reason?

No, I was not unfriendly. I distanced myself from everybody and everything because I took my job and the mission very seriously. To focus on my work, I practiced the Gandhian principle of self-denial and this helped me through the most difficult phases of my nine-and-half-year long tenure with the NBT

When you look back at your days in NBT, how would your describe them?

Most satisfying. My colleagues, especially the junior staff, rallied around me and I was able to channelise their time and energy for positive thinking and constructive work. I reciprocated their affection and respect and the rest is history. I still cherish a very special bond with the NBT staff.

Do cross-cultural marriages work? Why do you think they fail?

I cannot say they do not work. Even my new partner, Arundhati is from a different region. Things did not go right with my former wife because apart from being immature, we could not maintain the right balance between parenting, work, and relationship. I regret that the relationship suffered.

Do you keep in touch with your first family and children?

Yes, we do and meet practically every week. The best part is that Arundhati and my former wife have become great friends.

How and when did Scholastic select you?

It all happened due to my search of quality books for children. As Director NBT, I organised seminars with Asian and African speakers at Frankfurt in two consecutive book fairs. I was not aware that Dr Carol Sakoian from Scholastic Inc., also attended these. She met with me and over a period consulted me about the prospects of doing business in India. Meanwhile, my involvement with children's literature grew when UNESCO invited me to speak on 'Co-publishing' at UNESCO, Paris and at book fairs in Nairobi and Harare. Later, APNET gave me the unique honour of attending their reflection and planning meeting, as the only non-African publishing professional, at a game reserve in Kenya. Seeing that I was trying to involve inter-governmental agencies for producing better books for children of the South, Carol suggested that I could try doing it the Scholastic way and invited me to visit Scholastic in New York.

Scholastic, the company mission, the committed staff and the way they promoted books and reading impressed me. Most of all, I was overwhelmed by the sincerity and generosity of D R Robinson, the Chairman, President and CEO. Not wanting to lose the opportunity of making my dream come true, I agreed to move on from NBT.

How would you describe your experience of dealing with MNCs?

Scholastic was a company with a difference; a company with a heart. Scholastic developed books with tremendous love and respect for children. It was always a pleasure calling on and interacting with Mr Robinson. He is so kind that even now he gives us ample time to meet with him whenever we visit the Frankfurt Book Fair.

Now that you are a publisher yourself and are also friends with other publishers, NGOs and literary consultants, how are you handling such diverse areas simultaneously?

I see no conflict. On the other hand, I find it more rewarding because I firmly believe that partnerships are crucial for publishing success.

Your future plans for Arvind Kumar Publishers and A&A Consultants?

More books; still better books. We are on the right path but need to raise the level of our operations.

You have a strong network of friends and professionals and love to travel. Is this true?

I enjoy travelling for adventure and vacation, but not otherwise. Our business partners are kind. They do not make us visit them for clinching deals. I have honourable professional friends; I do not indulge in the give-and-take that "networking" entails.

You share a close relationship with some well-known authors. Share some of the experiences you had with them.

I am close to many authors and have pleasant memories of long relationships with them. Some of them we have published, but some we have not had the opportunity to publish. One such person is Krishna Sobti. She is our friend, but has not chosen us as her publisher. In our independent publishing, we are also very particular about our contractual obligations.

I understand that you wanted to participate in the recently held World Book Fair; why didn't you?

In fact, we missed the last date of applying for the stall. When I requested an NBT official to help find us space, Arundhati felt that it would be difficult for us to devote eleven days for the event. And that closed the chapter.

Anything that you liked or missed at the WBF?

I liked the fair for the large number of exhibitors and the hundreds and thousands of books they offered. Since I visited the fair only for business meetings, there was nothing that I found missing.

Do you see any change in the general reading habits/interests?

Dropping very rapidly, especially in Indian languages. Nobody seems to care that the languages are languishing.

You started your career with Hindi publishing and now after 18 years you have again come back to publishing; any reason?

I was exposed to publishing from the age of four and this is the only world I know and love. I re-entered independent publishing because we wanted to publish what we truly like. For example, we have recently published a book *Fair Play* by Munro Leaf that I first read at the age of nine. We intend bringing it out in all Indian (non-English) languages. It is a book that every child should read and every school and library should possess.

How would you describe a good book?

Difficult question. My long association with publishing has honed my skills and I know a good book when I come across one. To me, a good book should bring commercial success as well as mental satisfaction.

Are you writing your memoirs?

No, never. If I ever write, it will be with a touch of humour and sadness on the self-centered society we are creating.

Which role do you enjoy the most: being a publisher, an administrator, or a literary consultant?

Indeed a publisher, of quality books.

(Publishing Today, March 2008)

ASOKE K GHOSH
Managing Director
PHI Learning (Pvt.) Ltd.

Our STM books are accepted all over the world

You have achieved a memorable success in book publishing. How you happened to come into this profession?

My parent's influence in my formative years created in me an appetite for books. When I lost my father I was 11 years old, and came under the care of my maternal grandfather. I started growing among the many books written and published by my maternal uncle Dr Durga Das Basu, author of the legal multivolume classic Commentaries on the Constitution of India. Dr Basu, a leading expert on Constitutional Law, was a Judge in the Calcutta High Court and a National Professor of Constitutional Law. I began taking interest in his books and in course of time, started learning, proof reading, copy editing etc. by helping him in his work. Meanwhile, I completed my course in Printing Technology and Graphic Arts from Jadavpur University and my graduation at Calcutta University. Then I joined Times of India and there I learnt the many nuances of magazine and newspaper printing. This coincided with the formation of a publishing house in India by Prentice-Hall Inc. of USA, and I had the opportunity to meet Leo Albert, Chairman of Prentice-Hall International and its President, Kenneth Hurst. Thus, I made my entry in the new company, Prentice-Hall of India, to take care of its operations.

Can you recollect any experience of significance or memorable occurrence in your early years with Prentice-Hall of India?

I had a thrilling experience of working for a few days with the Founder and Chairman of Prentice-Hall Group of Companies,

Richard Prentice Ettinger who was also a Congressman in the US House of Representatives. I had also on many occasions worked with Leo Albert, as well as Kenneth Hurst here in India and in the USA.

As a founder member and Past President of the Federation of Indian Publishers, can you say something on its formation?

There had been no associations exclusively to take care of the interests and problems of publishers. The Federation of Publishers and Booksellers Association of India (FPBA) which was started in 1953 was predominantly for booksellers whose interest was focused more on book trading and importing. In the 1960's expansion in book publishing was phenomenal, both in terms of number of titles and in the emergence of new publishers. I still remember the meeting of stalwarts in book publishing like Shyam Lal Gupta, O P Ghai and D N Malhotra, where it was decided to form the Federation of Indian Publishers. In 1973 it started functioning with Shyam Lal Gupta as its first President. Soon thereafter FIP received the official recognition from the Ministry of Education and Foreign Publishers' Associations. International Publishers Association (IPA) sent its Secretary General and his team for a mandatory inspection and soon afterwards IPA gave recognition to FIP and also made FIP's office in New Delhi, as IPA's headquarters for Southern Asia It is interesting to know that the FIP headquarters building was inaugurated by IPA President Manuel Salvat who came specially for this purpose. The inauguration was attended by Prentice-Hall's Kenneth Hurst, and McGraw-Hill's Mead Stone and Stan Kendrick who also flew to Delhi for this occasion. It tells a lot about the young FIP's international standing.

You have been the Chairman of the Delhi Book Fair for long now. How is the fair contributing to the development of the book industry? What is your vision for it in the coming five years?

When Delhi Book Fair was started in 1995 its success picked up momentum each year and justified our expectations. We have been organising the book fair in air-conditioned halls, but the constraint now is that only a limited air-conditioned space is allotted to us. Now we are trying to get more space and it seems we will succeed. We must remember that Indian authorship is growing, as also the students, teachers, readers and institutions. We are making efforts to publicise the Fair more extensively within India and outside.

As the Chairman of Indian Reprographic Rights Organisation (IRRO), please give your opinion on its present position in the international field.

IRRO was established in 2000, and was registered in June 2002 as a Copyright Society under the Indian Copyright Act. At a historic meeting in Oslo in 1984, IPA and STM together formed the International Forum for Reproduction Rights Organisations (IFRRO). As Member of the Executive Committee of the IPA, and of its Copyright Committee and as Member of STM, I was the witness to the deliberations to establish IFRRO. It is a source of pride for us that IFRRO has recognised our IRRO by inducting us as its Member. Presently we are working for its awareness among the authors, publishers and institutions in the country. We have signed bi-lateral agreements with Japan, Argentina and others. With English being the widely used language in India and in the Indian publishing scenario, we need to sign agreements with UK and USA who are the most important English publishing countries. The Government of India is in a better position to publicise about this organisation and its services to all the concerned organisations of learning and research, like universities and other scientific, technical, medical and agricultural institutions. We are initiating certain measures and I hope it will be working in full swing in due course.

You were on the Executive Committee of IPA for a number of years and its Vice President for four years. What do you think have been the most important events during your tenure?

With the help of D N Malhotra and O P Ghai I was able to bring IPA Congress to India in 1992, but we had to work very hard and consistently for it. The IPA Congress in India was positively a success, and there were around 600 foreign participants who came to India. It was inaugurated by the President of India, Dr. Shankar Dayal Sharma, and His Excellency Mario Soares, President of Portugal was the Guest of Honour. I still remember, during his speech Dr. Sharma referred to my name as Emperor Asoka, and quipped that it was king Asoka who was the earliest Indian publisher, alluding to the emperor's edicts in public places for people to read! We were also excited when the Dalai Lama addressed the audience. At that time we saw many Chinese delegates walking out of the hall. In 1984 the IPA Congress was held in Mexico, and I was the co-chairman with Akiro Norita, Chairman, Sony Corporation in the session on electronic and digital publishing. There, Norita predicted that we would in future, have a compact disc in which all material could be stored; which later became a reality! In 1996, the IPA Congress was held in Barcelona where it celebrated the 100 years of IP For this event, the renowned and controversial writer, Salman Rushdie who was under threat from extremists, was brought in secretly to address publishers. His was one of the best ever addresses that I have listened to. During his address, he cited examples of India and lauded its democracy, heritage and culture. Another very important international event that I attended and addressed was the Hundred Years of Berne Convention organised at Heidelberg, Germany in 1986.

What are your views on the entry of Foreign Publishing Companies into India?

Our country has always welcomed publishers from all over the world. This is not new. In fact, soon after the independence many foreign publishers began coming to India and set up their publishing offices. Our own company started in the year 1963 in collaboration with one of the largest publishing houses of the US I do not see any problem in foreign publishing houses coming to India as long as they follow the rules and regulations of the country.

How many new titles and reprints do you publish each year?

In the last fiscal year we did 300 new titles and 725 reprints. The print run of each reprint varies from 1,000 copies to 30,000 copies. The expected trend is to produce more titles in the coming years.

Are you developing e-books? How has your experience been so far?

We started developing e-books with quite a few titles based on prospective demand. The initial response is encouraging. We are planning to do more e-books to cater to the emerging market.

Share your views regarding the export of Indian STM books to the developed and the developing world.

Our STM books are accepted all over the world. The quality of our content and production is at par with that of any good international publisher. To explore more into global markets, both in the developed and developing world, we have to invest enormously for promotion and product improvement consistent with their expectations. Please remember our scientific manpower is continuously increasing, and there are going to be more and more IIT's and other engineering colleges. Publishing and publishers' effort must also grow along with these.

You have been the Chairman of CAPEXIL Books Panel, you have been in the FIP's International Committee and also in IPA's International Committee. The export of books and print materials in 2008-09 was around Rs.1000 crores. On the global scale our share is practically insignificant. What will you suggest to increase book export to higher levels befitting the size of the Indian publishing?

We have to increase the publication of books immensely. The number of titles we export has a correlation with the number of titles produced. As I said just now, we need to spend more on promotion and content/product enrichment. Our government needs to give us support like UK does for their publishing. Book export of UK is the mainstay of the country's publishing industry. Their Government has established the British Councils all over the world which lend highest support to book promotion. It is not surprising that UK's book export is the highest for any country in the world and the industry prospers mainly on exports. The British Council's promotion of British books and the support given for book export are something that can be emulated by the Indian Government.

Have you started selling online? What has been your experience?

Yes, we are promoting and selling books online. We do this on our own from in-house facilities as well as through online agencies. The online promotion and selling is encouraging.

Do you prefer selling rights or are you in favour of marketing your own editions internationally?

We do sell rights in languages. However, we prefer to sell our own editions where it is required in English language as our prices are very reasonable.

How is your publishing house meeting the social responsibility towards society?

The very nature of our profession calls for meeting social responsibilities, particularly from the head of the publishing house. As a publisher, I take this responsibility seriously. I am a Kotarian, and I am also associated with other voluntary and charitable organisations. I have set up Rimjhim Ghosh Foundation in memory of my younger daughter for providing education, health care and other relief to the needy, especially the girl children. I have contributed, and continue to contribute towards the community, in the areas of health care, literacy, hunger alleviation, education and many other areas of need. They are numerous to list every item here. Above all, I am deliberately pricing our books lowest for the benefit of the economically weaker sections of society.

Do any family members help you in publishing?

My wife and daughter are fully involved in the operation and the management of PHI.

What would you consider a good book?

I feel a 'good book' must satisfy the objective – it should help the teacher to teach and the student to learn. This is also our mission statement. It must also be affordable in price, as otherwise it will be inaccessible and meaningless to the millions of students.

What are the new ideas you are introducing in PHI Learning?

The growth of the company depends on how well it can adopt new ideas. As the head of the organisation, I always like to adopt new ideas in order to expand my publishing programme. We try to be innovative in the matter of the content of the books, their presentation and marketing. This certainly requires team work. We are also trying to cover all the subjects and disciplines on which an academic publisher is expected to have books.

You have a number of tie-ups with international publishers, share your experience and how cooperation is mutually beneficial.

Yes, you are right. We have many publishing partners. As you know, the partners in business will always be there as long as mutual interest is looked after. Our partners are benefitting from their tie-up with us, just as we are benefitting from our association with them. Our partnership with all our international publishers is based on this quid pro quo, and this is what business is made of.

(Publishing Today, July-August 2009

BALRAM SIDHWANI

Director
UBS Publishers Distributors and
President
Bangalore Publishers & Booksellers Association

A good book gives directions to life and thinking

When UBS started a branch in Bangalore were you the first manager?

UBS started its first branch in Bangalore, in 1970 and I was the second manager to be appointed in December 1980.

When did you join UBS and why?

I did my B Com (Hons) from Shri Ram College of Commerce, Delhi and I saw my professors writing textbooks year after year, which were being used by the students extensively. Professor K P Sundaram a well-known author, was the in charge of NCC and I was also in NCC. I was influenced by him and wanted to join a book distribution company, so that I could also be an instrument in spreading education. There was an advertisement against which I applied and was selected. I joined as sales assistant in 1968. Later on, I was promoted and was made the sales manager of North India.

What new innovations you did when you were appointed as branch manager in Bangalore?

At that time our sales were 8-9 lakhs a month which is our per day sales now. UBS had also started their publishing programme. I started taking interest to develop new authors from South India, specially from Bangalore which helped us to increase our sales and our foothold in south India. We also started taking printing of school textbooks from the government of Karnataka, which helped us in establishing good relationships with the authority and we were printing without a printing press i.e. getting our books printed by outsourced. We also started identifying key booksellers who were good pay masters and honest in their dealings. With this our turnover increased. They became proud of us and we became proud of them. Even now 80-90% of the accounts we established are still working and are improving year after year. We have always encouraged them in institutional supplies and never overtaken them for short term gains. We have become dynamic wholesaler which has paid us very good dividends.

You strengthened Bangalore Publishers and Booksellers Association and started Bangalore Book Festival. How did you do it and how and when you established the book festival?

Around the year 2000 we, i.e. Ulhas Kumar, BI; Satish Venu, Satish Agencies; N Gangaram, Gangaram Book Bureau; Devru Bhatt, India Book House met and decided to strengthen the Association, so that we can give something to the industry. All of us agreed and they elected me the President and Devru Bhatt of India Book House as the Secretary in 2001 to give it a concrete shape. We decided to hold the Bangalore Book Festival, as it is being done in other cities of India. We outsourced the Book Festival to an agency called Club Class, giving them the responsibility for promotion, advertising, newspaper coverage and kept the participation with the Association. In return the Agency is giving a royalty to our Association. In the first few years they were investing, but now it has become a profitable venture for them. We kept a tight control over Club Class by giving them autonomy, keeping the working relationship mutually advantageous.

What is your Association doing for its members?

We help booksellers and publishers in many ways, such as:

a) We actively participate in the antipiracy activities by awareness drives and telling booksellers to keep only original books and not the pirated ones.

b) We organise publishing seminars from time to time in collaborations with the Federation of Indian Publishers and Booksellers Association in India for enhancing their education.

c) We help them in getting timely payment from the institutions. Recently Bangalore University was withholding the payment of the booksellers on the pretext that an audit is going on for seven months. We took up the matter and the payment was released making them understand that the industry needed their support by getting timely payments to give them better services.

d) We have started giving financial aid to the staff members of the Association for medical emergency and for education of their children. We have kept a special fund starting with Rs. 25,000/- which has been increased to Rs. 50,000/- this year.

e) Our booksellers from especially Sapna and Shankar have made us proud. Sapna by having a five storey bookmall which is the only one in India and Shankar by giving a personalised service has been able to spread their wings from a bookstall at the Bangalore airport to starting their branches at Westend Hotel in Bangalore; Thiruvananthapuram, Coimbatore, Cochin and now Nalanda at the Taj in Mumbai.

Have shopping malls killed the small/independent booksellers?

No. Both are surviving. Shopping malls have helped the regional language books by keeping a special section and displaying these prominently. The independent bookshops are giving a personalised service on a complementary basis which the shopping malls cannot afford to do.

What are your views on ebooks?

At the moment ebooks are not affordable, and volumes may not come very fast, but it has a lot of scope and once these become affordable, they will have their own place.

Has UBS any time thought of starting their own bookshops?

No. As we would like to develop our own portfolio and give a good service to the book industry.

Do you get time to read books?

Not much. I love to see T.V. programmes – spiritual, music, dance, and read newspapers and magazines on business.

You are in Bangalore for the last 30 years. Have you ever thought of learning Kannada language?

Once, I started learning keywords in Kannada and I met a person from Tamil Nadu. He said that I should not learn Kannada but Tamil and another person said I should learn Telugu and another Malayalam. So I thought it is better that I should stick to English only.

Have you ever thought of going back to Delhi?

I am not keen now and moreover I am happy being here. I have one son and a daughter. Both are married and well settled.

What do you think is a good book?

A good book should give directions to life and thinking.

What do you do to keep yourself happy and healthy?

I follow Baba Ramdev's yoga of breathing and warm up exercises which keeps me happy, fit and healthy.

(Publishing Today, April-May 2010)

BIPIN SHAH
Head
Mapin Publishing (Pvt.) Ltd.

Visibility is equally important as making new contacts

You are a successful Indian art publisher. Share with us your journey so far.

It's been a fascinating journey exploring the richness of Indian art and meeting creative people. Charting unexplored territory and documenting it has been especially gratifying.

From being a chemical engineer to a publisher? What made you enter publishing?

The roots of publishing were established in New York in the late '70s, soon after I graduated from the University of Wisconsin. It was during an extended holiday in India that turned the tide away from chemical engineering to publishing. Publishing seemed more exciting than chemical engineering and I haven't looked back ever.

You also worked in New York for a few years with a publishing house. Tell us about your experience there.

I worked with a small art book publisher learning the tricks of the trade. The experience at Doubleday's international division gave me the international exposure and the two together provided me with the vision required to build an international publishing company.

In 2005 you launched MapinLit and in 2007 you began the children's imprint. How has the response been and how many titles have you published in each?

MapinLit has not been very successful, although we have published about 20 plus titles. The children's books have taken off the ground well as it fits in more with Mapin's expertise. There are 4 titles in the market and 4 more will be coming into the market this fiscal year.

How many books do you publish in a year and what is the average print run?

We publish about 10 to 12 art books in a year and the average print run is 2500 to 3500 copies.

How do you market these books and how many sales staff and offices do you have?

We market through the usual wholesalers and retailers in the Indian market. Internationally, we use a pool of commissioned sales representatives through our stockists in the US and UK/Europe.

You work in close cooperation with international art book publishers and museums. Who all have you worked with and what kind of a relationship have you developed with them?

The international market has been our focus since our first book was published in 1985. It is through persistent focus on quality that we have established a reputation of being one of the best Indian art book publishers. We also develop products of interest for international publishers. Working with and establishing a relationship with international museums was not an easy task. We have focused equally on the content, editorial and design aspects and then finally on production. All three components are important. We have been associated with some of the best names in the industry – Abrams, Abbeville Press, Prestel, Smithsonian Institution, Rubin Museum, The Metropolitan Museum of Art, to name a few.

Tell us about your participation and experience in international book fairs.

Frankfurt Book Fair, Book Expo of America (BEA) and London International Book Fair are important book fairs. Visibility is equally important as making new contacts at these fairs. Book fairs also help create new ideas for publishing.

You once said in one of your interviews, "There is virtually no readership of our books." How many copies do you manage to sell in India and how many do you export on an average? Which has been your best seller?

India: Art & Culture has been our best seller. On an average the Indian market absorbs about 50% of the sales, however, the numbers have been shrinking over the years.

Art book publishing is an expensive venture. Do you tie up before publishing? Tell us how it works.

Yes, indeed; it is capital intensive to publish art books. Selection of subjects and timing are crucial. We try to co-publish with international publishers and museums, as far as possible. We also package books for international publishers.

Though Delhi is the book capital of the country, why did you choose Ahmedabad as the head office of Mapin?

Today with emails, high speed cable internet, mobile phones and blackberrys it really does not matter where you are. Having said that, travelling is important to meet people across the table and discuss ideas and learn from others.

What do you think has been the impact of globalisation on Indian publishing?

Globalisation has been good for Indian publishing. It offers us the opportunity to learn and connect with the international market. Indian publishing has made a limited impact on the international scene. We need to broaden our vision beyond our shores.

How is your working relationship with Mallika Sarabhai in running Mapin Publishing? How have you divided the work between the two of you? Who are the other family members who also help you?

Mallika Sarabhai and I started Mapin in 1985. She was fairly active for a number of years but now she contributes in a limited manner – by way of reading and editing manuscripts. Our son, Revanta who is trained in multimedia, occasionally designs books for Mapin.

What books do you like to read and are you planning to write your autobiography?

I enjoy serious non-fiction and poetry. Not everyone should write their biography and certainly not publishers!

How would you describe a good book?

A good book is one which opens a new window of your mind or brings in a fresh breeze of ideas.

(Publishing Today, October 2008)

CHIKI SARKAR
Editor-Publisher
Penguin India Books

Create an atmosphere for reading and writing

You joined Bloomsbury in 1999, after finishing your studies in UK. What was your subject of study?

Modern History and English.

Share your experience at Bloomsbury. What was your first assignment and how did you evolve in your role?

My first job would have been to photocopy manuscripts and make tea. I worked with Alexandra Pringle, the publishing director, for seven years and grew there eventually to become commissioning editor. It all happened very naturally. I was just given more and more responsibilities, as it happens in most companies.

From Bloomsbury, London, you joined Random House, India as Editor-in-Chief in 2006. Share your experience.

My five years at RHI are probably the most intense and memorable in my life. I had to start a list and give it an energy and identity very quickly. I didn't know anyone in Delhi, or in India, professionally before that – so it was setting up everything from scratch in a new place. And I always wanted to be different (which isn't always a good thing!) and which often led to trouble. But in my five years, RHI became the house of the most extraordinary new literary debuts. We created the entire health genre which RHI still leads on, and we published the most interesting lifestyle books from TV tie-ins like *Highway on my Plate* to stylish cookbooks like *Italian Khana*. Milee Ashwarya, who was the commissioning editor with me at RHI and who is now the publisher of Ebury, must be the most brilliant lifestyle editor in the country today.

Your memorable acquisition in fiction and non-fiction at Random House?

The literary debuts are all amazing and remain the publishing I love the most: Mohammed Hanif, Daniyal Mueenuddin, Basharat Peer, Namita Devidayal, Shehan Karunatilaka, Aman Sethi. Signing on Rujuta Diwekar was as high as was persuading IIMA to do a series of business books under their banner. Before I left, we got Suhel Seth to do an Indian version of *How to win friends and influence people* which has become a hit this year and tied up with Mint to do business books. All these were strong ideas and there's something very addictive about building a book from the idea up. We also reissued all the Anita Desai backlist when I first got to RHI and I think these editions of her books remain one of her favourites. Giving something old a new life and repackaging stuff is also another passion of mine.

Recently you joined Penguin India as an Editor-Publisher. What challenged you to undertake this move?

I couldn't say no – it was too good an opportunity.

You have worked in three international MNCs; is the work culture similar in all of them?

Penguin as a company is more international-minded, with lots of interactions between the other companies across the world. The different RH companies across the group are more insular. This is the main difference between the two, apart from their list. Bloomsbury was a small, stylish, independent group which has now grown with outposts in Germany, the USA and the UAE. It must be the only example of a company that is growing to be a sort of MNC, although much smaller in scale, but its DNA lies in very literary, high quality publishing.

Do you enjoy working day in day out with authors?

Love it, love it, love it. It's why I am here.

A bestseller in UK is usually guaranteed to be an international bestseller. An Indian bestseller is not so necessarily — what are your thoughts?

Absolutely! And nor is a Brazilian or a Japanese bestseller. And ofcourse, this doesn't relate just to books. It has to do with so many things; but in the simplest sense because of political structures, of US/UK being regarded and dealt with as the 'centre of things'.

You have worked with known authors. What have been your experiences? Any anecdotes?

I've loved working with all my authors, even the ones I've fallen out with subsequently. Every writer, even the unknown ones, have their quirks. I had a debut author once, who refused to do public appearances. Salman Rushdie, on the other hand, is the most publicity-savvy author, I have ever worked with. When we were discussing the publication of *The Enchantress of Florence*, he actually knew which specific journalists he wanted us to contact for the book and he was spot on. He's very smart and aware of the Indian media. The author I have had the hardest time working with is Anita Desai and it's because she doesn't use email! You have to fax or mail her stuff and in the age of internet, let me tell this can be exhausting. It's made up by the fact that she writes lovely notes even when they're about banal matters and I used to save them up.

How do the large multinationals manage selling of rights amidst themselves in different territories and outside?

Well I think you do this by building relationships with editors across the company, so you know what kind of book they like and who to pass things on to. I did a lot of that at RHI and have started doing this at PBI. Making friends all around the world with fellow editors is one of the most fun things about my job. I've always loved it.

How would you describe a good book?

Tough question. It depends. For a literary book, I judge the prose and the ambition. I also often now buy a literary book thinking I am not just buying one book but a writer, who I want to take a bet on. For a commercial book, it is the idea and how much it grips me. But you know what its really about? When I read a manuscript, and I think its special, for whatever reason, two things happen. First: as I read it, my heart starts beating really fast, it's as if I had a crush. I can also often see exactly how to do it, how to pitch it, how it should look etc. Secondly, I find myself talking about it afterwards. Everywhere – at work, at dinner parties, on the phone with friends. Then I know it's sunk inside me and it is love.

Your views on globalisation and its impact on Indian publishing?

Well this is such a large question, I am not exactly sure what it means. Do you mean the role of MNC's in Indian publishing? In which case, I would say, it's been stimulating – from OUP to Penguin, international companies have published extraordinary books in India and nurtured great talents alongside our brilliant Indian houses.

Do you think print publishing will die or perish with the onslaught of digital publishing in the next five years?

Well, I certainly think there will be a time in the future that there will be more ebooks than print books. I don't think this is doomsday though.

What is your opinion regarding royalties on printed book verses digital book.

The current royalties on ebooks are much higher than printed books – most international publishers pay 25% net receipts and I think this is largely a matter of consensus. The larger question is, "will those ebook royalties increase and to what extent?"

What are your hobbies and how do you spend your spare time?

I am very boring. I read a lot. I love to cook and eat and run, watch movies, go to plays, and concerts and art shows. I love travelling and am often heading off somewhere or the other. Really run of the mill I am afraid.

What are your views on the copyright amendments for which the bill is under consideration in the Parliament?

The proposed amendment as you know has now been dropped – and along with all my fellow publishers who campaigned against it, I am extremely happy that this has happened.

How would you rate the social responsibility of a publisher, and how is Penguin meeting the same?

To get people reading more books. To create an atmosphere where people will want to write more. Its PBI's 25th birthday next year and we are going to be introducing all sorts of exciting new campaigns around this which you'll hear more of later on.

(Publishing Today, December-January 2012)

DHANESH JAIN
Managing Director
Ratna Sagar (Pvt.) Ltd.

Competition is good for growth

You started Ratna Sagar in 1982, when you were a Professor of Linguistics. What prompted you to start an educational publishing house?

I was teaching at JNU when I thought of changing track. The salary hardly supported my petrol bills. Money was one factor. So I resigned from JNU. I joined my family business of buttons and started a button factory in 1976. Soon I found I had a lot of spare time from the factory. I started Ratna Sagar so that I could again be with the academic world. Here, my friend's brother Ashok Zutshi, who was working with a publishing house, also joined me. This is how Ratna Sagar came into being. The button business is still being run by the family.

How did you select the name Ratna Sagar?

It is named after one of the three grand libraries of the ancient Nalanda University (1500 years ago). So you could say that we have a 1500-year-old name in the world of books.

What were the initial publications of Ratna Sagar?

We started with children's and school textbooks. We worked on a series of science books 1-5 in four colour which was not common at that time. This was our first major publication. A lot of work went into the making of these books and took us more than three years to bring out 5 books. Eventually, this became a landmark in textbook publishing and even after twenty-five years it is still considered a market standard.

Recently you started a dictionary division and joined hands with Collins of UK. How are the arrangements going on?

We are pleased to join hands with HarperCollins India and promote their dictionaries. We started with 3 dictionaries last year and have a range of seventeen Collins dictionaries this year.

You have a well established marketing network in India. Which was your first branch office in India? Are you planning to go overseas?

We have billing branches in Delhi, Lucknow, Chennai and Kolkata. Besides, we have 14 offices spread all over India. We do plan to go overseas. Already our books go to South Asia.

Getting books adopted in schools is not a clean business. How you are overcoming this or are you following the accepted norms?

It's a difficult option and gets you into a lose – lose position either way.

You have also started an Academic Division for Libraries recently though the sales to Libraries is also not a clean business. What has been your experience?

Being an academic myself, I am attached to academic publishing and sentimentally would love to be in the company of academics. I have been a general editor for the Motilal Banarsidas Series in Linguistics. I know there aren't big revenue possibilities in this, but as my heart is in this, so we have started an imprint Primus Books. We are publishing academic books in history and have also joined hands with Byword Books to publish medical books.

What is the buzz word in Ratna Sagar?

Excellence. Pursuit of excellence. We are very conscious about the quality of our product and our mission statement also states the same. We are in education and consider it lesser of a business and more of a mission.

Do you find time to read and what do you normally read?

Sure, I do. I am a student of linguistics and pursue the subject of my training. I have co-edited a volume on *Indo-Aryan languages* which has been published by Routledge, UK. I had to take time out of my work to work on this volume. It took us three years to finish it. I left the work at Ratna Sagar on Auto-Pilot and with persons like Atiya Zaidi around Ratna Sagar, I did better in those years than in earlier years.

How do you describe a good book?

Excellence again though many regard sale as a major criterion. Our books are oriented towards learning and not examination. They help the child to understand the subject and not just pass an exam. So in my opinion a good book is a tool for learning.

Where would you like to see Ratna Sagar in the next 5-10 years?

We have been growing at 30% + every year. We would like to diversify further into areas of education and learning.

Are you developing ebooks and online teaching?

It is a long process and we are open to it. My son, Sugat Jain has joined the business. He is a software technocrat. We have started working towards it by providing web support through dedicated websites. Many of our books have interactive CD's.

When Macmillan acquired Frank Bros in 2006 what was your reaction? There were rumours that Ratna Sagar is next on the line?

Mergers and acquisitions are a routine in the corporate world. But Ratna Sagar is not up for grabs.

Which role you enjoy the most — Professor/Teacher/Author or a Publisher?

All. By training I am an academic, by profession a businessman and by choice an author.

What are your views on Nationalisation of Textbooks upto school level?

We know competition is good for growth but in this sector not much growth has taken place. When all other areas are opening up, why not this sector as well? The government should open this sector up totally.

What are your views on globalisation and the role of MNC's in India in the context of publishing?

Globalisation has been a part of publishing for the last hundred years in India, as we have been importing books and there is no duty, Indian publishers are also exporting and there are no constraints. Multinational publishing houses are here for more than a century. They have survived along with the locals. So it is not something new.

Do you think print media will be overtaken by digital media in the times to come?

Digital media is growing rapidly and has already taken ten to twelve per cent of the market share in the US. However, both will survive as these are just different delivery methods of content.

(Publishing Today, February-March 2010)

GANDHI KANNADHASAN
Managing Director
Kannadhasan Pathippagam

Website is an investment and not an expense

Kannadhasan, I learnt that your father was a very learned author and publisher. Can you tell us how he started and from where you took over?

My father, late Poet Laureate Kannadhasan, was a well known Tamil poet. He studied only till the 8th standard and read most of the books of Tamil literature. He contributed 8,000 film lyrics, 3,700 poems and 267 books. He was a journalist and publisher of a weekly, daily and also books.

He started the company KANNADHASAN PATHIPPAGAM to publish his works. And when I was studying law in 1976 I took over the company, as the law college was only held in the morning.

When you came into publishing, was it your own initiative or at the insistence of your father?

It was my interest and my father encouraged and supported me. He also taught me how to proofread and edit manuscripts.

You are a well established Tamil publisher. Please let us know about your publishing house and what kind of books you publish?

We are in the process of establishing ourselves. We have four branches, strategically located in Madurai, Coimbatore, Puducherri (Pondicherry) and Vellore. Our overseas branches are in Singapore and Malaysia. We are concerned about translation in those countries. By 2010 we will have three more branches and God willing, two more overseas.

As you are one of the progressive Tamil publishers, an exporter, and have two offices outside India, please let us know how the inspiration came to you to start the offices and how successfully are the overseas operations going on?

As book publishers we are all fortunate that we are welcome wherever we go. As part of the Knowledge Industry we are more respected than those from other industries. My experience proves this. And our overseas branches are focused not on marketing what we have, but on what we can get from there and on giving them what they want. Hence, the market is very friendly and gives us a lot of feedback. We are still in the investing stage and returns are expected from the next financial year. There is a very good Tamil population overseas and my father commands a lot of respect from them. So the support already exists and all I have to do is to channelise it.

You are the President of Booksellers and Publishers Association of South India (BAPASI). Please let us know when you took over this post and what are the initiatives you have taken to improve the lot of the Tamil publishing industry?

I became the President of BAPASI in 2006, unopposed. The Tamil publishing industry was growing and the support from the government is enormous. I merely stood between the industry and the government and things happened.

1. A Bookpark in Chennai for all the Publishers and Booksellers in Tamil Nadu. Land has been provided free by the government and State Bank of India (SBI) has underwritten the project of building. The process of allotment is on and every publishing group in the association will get a space in the park.
2. The government is setting up a Publishers' Welfare Board and the budget of 2008-09 allocated funds for it. It will be active by October 2009. We want to include binders also in this segment as they do not have an association.

3. The state library movement was buying 600 copies of a title of Tamil books for their libraries. And our Honourable Chief Minister M Karunanidhi, increased the number of copies to 1,000.
4. The CM also increased the good books and authors award by the Tamil Nadu government to Rs 10,000 for the publisher and Rs 20,000 for the author.
5. During the inauguration of the 30th Chennai Book Fair in 2007, our beloved CM gave one crore rupees to BAPASI, from his personal funds to create an endowment in his name and for giving cash awards of rupees one lakh each to four Tamil authors, one author from other Indian languages and one author hailing from India, who writes in English.
6. Directorate of Rural Development is establishing 12,000 libraries in all village panchayats. The first phase of book purchase of 5,165 titles has already been done; and the next phase is on. The purchase ratio is 85% Tamil books and 15% English books.
7. On our request our beloved CM had issued a Government order to allot two book kiosks at each bus stand to sell Tamil books in Tamil Nadu. One will be allotted on first come first serve basis and another on the recommendations of BAPASI. All the corporations, municipalities and panchayats had been issued this G O. More than two hundred had come up and many more are in the process. Estimated 1,800 to 2,500 shops may come up by June 2010.

I am indeed very happy to say that all this happened during my tenure as President of BAPASI.

Under BAPASI you organize the Chennai Book Fair. Please share with us when it began and how it has come of age?

Pioneers of BAPASI like K Krishnamurti, A Padmanabhan, K V Matthew, A Abdulla, N A V Subramanian, S Chandrasekar and many more are the pillars of the Chennai Book Fair (CBF). We had a very tough time in promoting the Fair. BAPASI started in 1972 and the CBF in 1977.

We began conducting the Fair with 20 participants, even in drive in restaurants. In 1985, we shifted the venue to Arts College on Mount Road and the fair grew. In 2007, in my tenure as the President, we felt the need to grow and moved to the present venue at St George's School on Poonamalle High Road with 525 stalls and the 32nd CBF 2008 saw 630 stalls in over one lakh square feet area, with a sale of around 15 crore rupees.

You are politically very well connected with the Chief Minister and I learnt that he gave you a corpus grant. How do you utilize the same? Do you give any awards to promote professionalism in publishing?

As I have already explained we do not have an award as you had asked. But you have given me a very good idea. We honour the veterans of this industry but have no awards for professionalism. Thanks for the idea!

How do you rank yourself in Tamil literary publishing? How many new titles and reprints do you publish each year?

I am walking on a very comfortable path. The path was laid by the hard work of the earlier generation publishers, many decades ago. They had cleared all the obstacles and hardships. All I do is walk and run. Our strength is in reprints. This numbers more than our new releases. We release around fifty new books every year.

What is your policy on vanity publishing? Do you encourage it? If so, how many such books do you publish in a year?

As far as vanity publishing is concerned, it is born out of the ego of the writer. Because money or influence or power is involved, the publisher takes it up. But the reader knows and does not buy. So the Government buys out of the influence of the author or the publisher. So an opportunity for a good book is lost. This will be the last thing I will do as a publisher.

Do Tamil publishers use ISBN and barcoding? What effect has it had on the business?

Yes, we have started using the barcode and ISBN. The process has just begun and the effects are not visible yet.

How many new Tamil language books are being published annually?

As we submit to the state library, the statistics are available from there and also from the submissions made to Delhi Public Library under the Delivery of Books Act. The mandatory requirement for our submission is around 4,500 to 5,800 titles annually.

What is the impact of globalisation on Tamil language publishing?

Orders from abroad and dealership enquiries. Tamil authors from abroad are keen on having their writing published here as well as in their country they are residence of. New authors, multinational players and Indian players want to enter the Tamil book publishing industry. Already Westland-Tata has come out with two titles of Sir Jeffrey Archer and he himself released the Tamil translation of his book in Chennai a few days ago. Communication with publishers abroad and authors has become effective and fast. They have started to believe in Indian enterprises.

How do you think shopping mall culture has increased the sale of regional language books?

Yes, Landmark has two shops in two malls in Chennai. And they are doing well. They sell Tamil books in good quantity. Tamil books have a separate display area and it is wonderful to find people browsing through them along with English books.

Many Tamil people are settled abroad. Do they help in the export of Tamil language books?

Yes, definitely. It is because of them that Tamil movies are released at the same time throughout the world. And they also import books. But there is no organised distribution network or organised retail. So, we are trying to organise this distribution and retailing. When this is in place, for export alone to the UK, Switzerland, Norway, Denmark, France, Singapore, Malaysia and Australia we will have to increase our print run by 5,000 copies.

How is your publishing house meeting the social responsibility towards society?

We do certain things that are best left unmentioned, as there will not be much value in what we do or have done, if we publicise it. But to motivate others we mention a few. Our central prison needed books and all our titles have been given free of cost and all new releases reach them likewise. We have adopted three rural non-profit libraries and we send ours, as well as other books to them.

We take care of our employee's children and their education. We are trying to give back to this society as this society supports us by buying our books.

Tell us something about your website and online selling.

Our website is helping us to introduce us to our overseas buyer and rights sellers. Nothing much; no online trading as our books are low priced. But a website is an investment and not an expense. The goose is waiting to lay golden eggs. All we need is patience.

Do any family members help you in publishing? Also, do you find time to indulge in reading for pleasure? If so, when, and which is the last book you read?

My son Murali Kannadhasan is engaged with me in this business and sits next to me. He is an MBM from Victoria University, Australia.

He likes to publish, though he reads lesser and lesser. But reading will catch up with him I suppose. Yes, reading is for pleasure. I loved reading the book, *The Secret*, and I would love to publish it in Tamil. But this comes second. Reading has made me what I am now. Recently I read Sir Archer's book translated in Tamil. Good translation and well produced. Westland-Tata had done it. I wish all good books in English could be made available in Tamil as the man in Kanyakumari also needs it.

What would you consider a good book?

Every book is a good book. As the author who had penned it certainly contributed something there that will be of your interest. But we do not have the patience to read till we find what we want. It has to be on the first page. When I was a boy, *Jonathan Livingston Seagull* by Richard Bach was a talked about book. I read it without being able to understand it. But I underlined some lines. I am surprised that they reflect now in my life. All books are good. I love the pictorial edition of *Kamasutra*. Books are a part of my life.

What is the controversy regarding the copyright of your father's works with the state government?

This I want to forget and I know that I cannot. Our core strength is my father's books, hence our cash bills are more than credit bills. My father passed away in 1981. One fine day I saw in the evening papers, that the Tamil Nadu Government wanted to nationalise the writings of my father. I strongly condemned the move and issued statements in papers and television channels. The Honourable Chief Minister was shocked to see this and issued a rejoinder and the move was dropped.

I was wrong in going to the press. When the CM treats me like one of his sons and has given me all the support and encouraged me to do what all I wanted, for the publishing industry, I had done him a wrong. This guilt will live with me forever.

He is like a godfather to me. And I am one of the very few who call him Appa, which means father. I should have gone to him and told him about the move. His love for me is so much that he calls me by my name wherever he sees me. When he talks to me he always mentions some of the incidents he shared with my father.

This is what happens, when you are emotional and there are no elders at home to guide you. I miss my elders so much.

(Publishing Today, June 2009)

GEETA DHARMARAJAN
Founder and Executive Director
KATHA

Start day with prayer and end it with prayer

Share with us your journey from how you got involved in NGO work to becoming a successful publisher.

I belong to a middle class family and we are three sisters and a brother and lots of aunts and uncles and temples and riverine villages filled with stories apocryphal and immediate, imagined and real. When I was about 8 years old, my father took me to Higginbotham's, Madras to reward me for a painful tooth extraction. He gave me ten rupees to buy any book I wished for. Ten whole rupees! I remember buying *King Arthur's Legends,* my first book in English, and enjoying it immensely. Story and storytelling have always been important in my life for as long as I can remember. I remember going to the temple and listening to stories, practically every night. In 1970 I got married to Raju [K Dharmarajan]. In 1977, he was posted in the Nilgiris. Being the wife of a District Collector, I was elected director of Women's Voluntary Services. Giving back to society was something I had learnt from my father and this just somehow seemed the right thing for me to do, too. Then, stints in publishing — with the India Today Group, with the *Target* magazine and Rosalind Wilson and at the University of Pennsylvania [USA] – brought me into publishing and design. After my return to Chennai in 1985, I was invited to be director, education for the Indian National Trust for Art, Culture and Heritage (INTACH) till 1987. One more transfer for Raju saw me back in Delhi and Katha began in our garage in 1988. I started with *Tamasha!* — a children's story magazine. And soon I was running a library from our garage for children studying in the local government school. Katha was registered as a charitable society in 1989, serendipitously on September 8, World Literacy Day — thus giving the tone and culture to the organisation and reiterating the mission goal: to enhance the joys of reading.

You have three passions in life: being wife and mother, helping children gain an education, and publishing. How do you pursue them all with enthusiasm?

Anything that is interesting and fun to do becomes easy to do, right?

Can you explain how all your activities revolve around STORY telling?

When story is everywhere around us — in the media, TV ticker tapes, gossip at the bus stand — it is not difficult to remember that most ancient civilisations spread their ideas and philosophy, what they lived by and for, through story. In India, I learnt everything worth remembering through story. And as a grownup, I cannot think of anything better than story to enhance the joys of reading! We are moving with great speed from an oral to a written tradition, but the means remain the same: story! In Katha, the story research and resource centre informs our publishing and education activities. In fact if we have 8000 children in the Katha Schools today and 9000 women associated in our activities, and if we have a very low single-digit dropout rate [compared to about 75% elsewhere], I would say, it is owing to the strength of story. And our pedagogy: story pedagogy®.

When Katha was born you published a book a year. How many books are you doing now?

We started with the annual volume of Katha Prize Stories with translations from amongst 21 Indian languages. Our yearly output at the moment is 5 to 6 books for adults and 20 to 25 books for children, in English and in Hindi.

You publish books in series. How many series do you have and how do you develop them?

Our series start with the Katha Prize Stories and include graded readers for children and young adults. We have an academic series — the studies in culture and translation series — *Translating Partition/Caste/Desire/Power* etc. We have a series of biographies including the *Life and Times of Ismat Chughtai*. We work with stories for children and adults.

Most of the books you publish are compiled by unknown authors. How do you market these books?

Our authors are well known in the Indian languages and by publishing them in English, Katha has tried to give them and their stories the visibility they deserve and bring translations on par with Indian writing in English. Our annual anthology, containing prize winning stories from different Indian languages, is eagerly awaited by connoisseurs of literature.

You give special attention to your covers and get them designed from well-known artists. How do you afford them?

Yes, our covers feature some of India's best loved painters, including some of our most admired friends like Tyeb Mehta, Anjolie Ela Menon, Jatin Das. Most of the covers are designed by me, and since I've developed good relations with most of our best artists, they have become a part of the Katha family, and so the question of money does not arise; however, Katha does give love and respect — and a small honorarium.

Katha being a successful NGO what do you think is the one factor which has contributed to your success?

Children, children and children! We provide our children with a joyful learning environment to grow and learn. Our alumni are now earning up to Rs. 200,000 per year! Last year they brought in 45 million rupees for their families. And our women earn about 40,00,000 per month. We have believed that when women earn, children get an opportunity to learn; and this has been the organisation's strength. We have driven our work on a single powerful idea, that children can help their communities get out of poverty through education. At the moment we have 8000 of our own children in Katha's quality schools in Delhi and Arunachal Pradesh, besides the 70,000 children who are part of the Katha Reading Campaign. The Delhi government invited Katha to help their 2.4 million children mission in 3000 schools by 2012 and bring greater reading skills to them and their 60,000 teachers.

Are the books developed by KATHA used only by your schools or do others use them as well?

Katha Schools do not have textbooks. The children have storybooks that bolster their reading habits; and teachers create their own teaching/learning materials in maths, science and other traditional and nontraditional subjects. Normally, the Katha Schools use Katha's storybooks. Katha's books are also regularly used in a large number of other schools – government, non-profit and private schools.

How was Katha successful in weaning away children from child labour and getting them enrolled into schools? Did you face any impediments?

I started a school in a large slum cluster in 1990. Today we have weaned more than 50,000 children away from labour. And more than 41,000 children since 2001 have earned computer certification from Katha InfoTech and eCom School. Over the last few years, our students have gone to college and are working in various places including IBM, Citibank, Delhi Government, Government of India etc., and supporting their families in sustainable ways! I have always believed that children stay with something that interests and feeds their natural sense of curiosity and desire to know their world. And this "inducement" is what has brought all our children into school and kept them with us so they pass the formal school leaving certificate exams. We believe in creating global citizens who can be at par with the world, not just adults struggling at the edge of poverty like their parents. And for this, quality is important. There were many difficulties, but none so special that they stopped me from doing what I knew I had to. And we had passionate, driven teachers — women from the communities we work in — and parents and elders who have helped make the journey pleasant and possible!

You have done commendable work helping children and communities get out of poverty. How did this idea come to you and what was the driving force behind it?

If parents are living in poverty they will not send their children to schools. To enable the children to come to us, we work with the mothers and help them to earn a living. When mothers earn, children learn. The Katha staff and students took a pledge in 2000: No child in Katha will live in poverty. And believe it or not, collective action has led to mass collaborations and innovative, creative ways in which our families can live with dignity and decency.

How and at what level are you working with the Government of Delhi?

After witnessing our track record, the Government of Delhi invited us to work in their 3000 schools. Initially, we have started work in 200 schools, plus 100 municipal corporation [MCD] schools. Our 500 - odd volunteers this year have been constantly working with students in these schools. In accordance with our agreement, we begin working with the children at the class three level and help build their vocabulary to 600 words — a Grade 3 reading level. I believe with this minimal skill, students should be able to scale to the next level with Katha. It has taken a lot of time to get things moving, but we got extremely good support from the CM of Delhi as well as from the Education Department people at various levels.

What do you think will be the impact of globalisation on the Indian publishing industry?

I feel that it will create a better distribution system for the industry and help it achieve better and higher standards. This will strengthen and consolidate the industry as a whole and having gained this collective strength, the Indian publishing industry will be unbeatable. Publishing is a creative field and will benefit from the borderless world created by globalisation.

Where would you like to see KATHA after 5 years?

We would like to touch 80 percent of children living in urban poverty in India; create books for them and help make a difference in their lives.

Do you get time to read?

I love reading and do a lot of it — though not as much as I would like! — fiction, non-fiction and translations.

How would you describe a good book?

It should keep me turning the pages, tell me a good story and have style. The Wah! feeling in a reader is important — for all stories worth the telling, I am told, were told in the Mahabharata! It should also be well designed so as to entice me to pick it up.

What comprises your typical working day?

I start my day with prayer and end it with prayer. During the day I am a volunteer for Katha, doing as well as I can whatever is expected of me.

(Publishing Today, January 2009)

J P VIJ

Managing Director
Jaypee Brothers Medical Publishers (Pvt.) Ltd.
Head, Jaypee Medical International and
Jaypee Pharma Customised Imprints (Pvt.) Ltd.

No competition in the field of medical publishing

You are one of the leading medical publishers in Asia. Tell us about the journey?

It all started way back in 1950 when my father, Late Sohan Lal Vij, started Vij and Rama Publishing House in Ludhiana where he began publishing technical books. He went through a lot of ups and downs during his lifetime. In 1957 he published a large number of Engineering textbooks and unfortunately the syllabus changed as a consequence of which he had to wind up his business and join Atmaram & Sons as production manager in Delhi. In 1969, my father (founder) and I (co-founder) decided to try our luck a second time and we re-established our publishing business. Thus was born Jaypee Brothers. But as fate would have it, in 1972 my father passed away from a heart attack at a young age of 48. I was only 16 years old then and was working and pursuing my graduation through correspondence from Delhi University. But I did not give up and my hard work and patience paid off. We now have 10 offices in India and this year started an office in St. Louis, US Our US office looks after the promotion and acquisition of manuscripts.

What made you opt for medical publishing?

In 1969, when we started Jaypee Brothers, there was no competition in the field of medical publishing and also there was a huge demand for books on hygiene, public health, and other allied subjects. This is what prompted us to take up medical publishing and so far we have been very comfortable in pursuing this specialty and can boast of around 250 titles in a sub-specialty area like ophthalmology alone.

What areas of operations do you look after?

I basically take care of the US and UK markets to interact with top international publishers for joint ventures and other future plans. Back home I am the planner of the organisation.

Which is a winner—publishing, importing or distribution of medical books?

Of course publishing; however, we do import a large quantity on an exclusive basis from McGraw Hill (USA), Hodder Arnold (UK) and FA Davis (USA).

How many new titles do you publish in a year and what was your major title in 2007?

We publish around 300 titles in a year. Some of the titles are selling in large quantities of upto 50,000 copies. There are a large number of titles which are really selling excellently in this part of the world.

Which was your first medical book published?

We published *A Guide to Pathology* in 1969. The book was written by a student and for students, and the book is still going strong and the author revises it as the need arises.

Does your list focus on text books for medical students or on reference books for doctors?

Both. We have a wonderful mix of text and reference. We have recently launched a video atlas containing DVDs related to various medical specialties.

Do the publishers you import from help in marketing your books in their countries?

Yes, certainly. McGraw Hill, Lippincott Williams and Welkins, Hodder and Anshan distribute our titles on a selective basis in their countries. We also distribute some titles of Lippincot Williams and Welkins, Springer, Taylor & Francis on a nonexclusive basis in India.

Have you developed any e-medical books? Tell us about your experience.

We are in the process of developing e-books in India. Our many books carry CDs/DVDs, and some books which are on-line are updated quarterly. Whatever books McGraw Hill distributes in the US are also converted shortly into e-books by them.

You also publish medical journals. Tell us something about these.

At this time we have only three journals but we plan to increase to six in the coming year. Our journal, *Ultrasound in Obstetrics and Gynaecology* has editors from Croatia and the US.

Do you have doctors on your editorial board? Do they help you in selecting titles?

Yes, we have three doctors on our role. They help us with the editorial and also in sorting out the queries of our editors.

Do you prefer selling rights or are you in favour of marketing your own editions internationally?

Whenever an English edition has to be sold, we prefer to sell our edition; otherwise, we are aggressive in selling translation rights in languages like Spanish, Chinese, Portuguese, Turkish, Arabic, Polish etc., and have signed many agreements.

Do you pay an advance against royalty to the authors or is it a one-time payment?

We do not prefer to pay advance royalty to the authors and neither are we interested in a one-time payment. We work purely on royalty percentage with the authors.

What is the percentage of domestic sales to exports? Which are your major export markets?

Our major market is the domestic market and we have 80% sales in India and our exports are 20% of the total sales. However, the US and UK, Malaysia, South-East Asia are our major export markets.

What special efforts do you do in marketing?

We organise international sales conferences in India every year where publishers from UK, US, Germany and other places participate and share their new programs for the year with our sales team.

Any plans to go public?

Yes, maybe in a couple of years as the situation demands.

Any new developments at Jaypee?

Recently, we opened our new office at the publishers' hub at Ansari Road, which is equipped with all the latest technology. We have also started a company, AJR Medi Solutions—publish effortlessly by outsourcing. The plan here is to take from the small publisher his burden and supply him with edited and printed books directly to his warehouse, as we, the bigger players have a better and suitable infrastructure to do this. The process includes, editing, pre-press, post-press, processing, data digitalisation etc.

In this age of acquisitions and mergers how is medical publishing fairing?

We have already initiated the process of acquiring small medical publishers in India and have recently added to our list, Arora Medical Publications, Lucknow. They have around 46 titles which are selling quite well in the market.

What price did you pay for this acquisition?

I would not like to divulge into the details at this moment.

Do you face any competition in medical publishing in India?

Not much. Most of the old publishers have now stopped publishing. They were previously based in Kolkata and Mumbai. We are now basically facing competition from the foreign publishers as they are reprinting their books at a low price in the Indian market. But this competition is very minor and does not affect our list.

How would you describe a good book?

That's a difficult one. I think the book which sells well and gives a real sense of satisfaction to the author, editor, and publisher that their efforts have borne fruit is in my opinion a good book.

Do you find time to read and if so what is your preference?

Let me share my 'browsing fascination' with you. I browse through each and every book of mine. I am always excited when a new book comes and cannot sleep till I have browsed through each page of the book.

Do your family members help you with your business? Also let us know about your family life and how do you enjoy your leisure time?

My wife, Raman Vij, is the director of the company and she looks after what the ladies like best – finance. She is a real motivation in my life. My son is doing graduation in publishing from Oxford Brooks in UK and will be joining me, shortly. I intend to send him for post graduation in publishing at the Imperial College, London in September 2008. He has already worked with Elsevier and Hodder Arnold for 6 months in UK.

How was the idea to organise a cricket match during the World Book Fair conceived?

I was in UK with Philip Walter, Managing Director of Hodder Arnold and was discussing about our business plans when every 5 minutes he would go and check the score of an ongoing cricket match. He obviously was an avid cricket follower. I am also very fond of cricket and so we planned to organise a cricket match between Indian and foreign publishers at the time of the World Book Fair. That is how this cricket match idea was conceived and now it seems to be a regular feature at every New Delhi World Book Fair.

(Publishing Today, May 2008)

KAMAL AHUJA

Director
Impulse Marketing

Always remember the best is yet to come

You are a successful direct marketing professional. How and when did you enter this field and how has your journey been so far?

I was in my final year of graduation, B.Sc. (Hons) Statistics at Delhi University, when by sheer luck I was selected as a door-to-door salesman by a wholesale warehousing company. They were dealing in all types of products including children's books. It turned out to be an interesting vocation and I started concentrating more on this rather than my studies. I was doing fairly well when I was asked to shift to Kolkata in 1994. So I left Delhi with Rs 200 in my pocket and went to Kolkata. Life was tough but interesting, which kept me excited. I moved to Bhubhaneshwar in early 1995 and was made a distributor. This resulted in not appearing for my final year exams. By 1996 I was successful in opening four more branches/distributors in Orissa. During this time the company started importing goods from China which were of an inferior quality and thus started the downward trend in the company and it finally wound up its operations in the year 2000. It was during this time that six of us – Som, Sanjay Bakshi, Manish Anand, K N Shaji, Sanjay Chowdhury and myself who had become close friends, decided to form our own partnership concern. Som moved to Delhi and I stayed back in Kolkata. In between I also went to Bangladesh for four months (where I lost 8 kgs!). We started marketing dictionaries, encyclopedias and children's books and the rest is history. All kinds of qualities are required to make a successful businessperson but aggressive single mindedness is the foremost requisite to be successful! This single mindedness was shared by us all.

Share with us the methodology of your working.

We go to people individually, show our product and then sell it. We have a network of 180 distributors having around 4000 salesmen who take 10 to 15 copies of a title and go to the people. Our main work is to motivate the distributors who in turn motivate the salesmen. Our offices start at 8.30 am, followed by the training session from 8.30 to 10.30. All salesmen are out in the field by 11 am and are back by 6.30 pm, for a debriefing session from 6.30 to 8.30 pm, where each salesman then presents his daily report. We are what we are today, not because of what we do today, but because of what all we have done in the last ten years.

What is the selection process for recruitment in your organisation? Are the marketing persons on a salary or commission or both?

None of our employees are on salary. We work on a commission basis. We are always on the look-out for ambitious people who are ever ready to learn and grow. It is our belief that if you want to succeed you will actually start succeeding!

You do not market to trade. Any particular reason?

We were conceived as a direct marketing company and our strength lies in training and motivating salesmen and reaching out to the people.

What is the ratio of fixing the MRP of a title to cost?

We believe in generating higher sales and keeping our margin to the minimum. We give 50 percent discount to the customer; 10 percent of the net price goes to the salesman, 15 percent to the distributor and 12.5 percent is given to the Head Office.

To which countries do you export your products and what marketing strategy do you follow there?

The distributors who have been successful with us in India are moved to different markets. We have our distributors in

Nepal, Bangladesh, UAE, Philippines and Sri Lanka. It is our own team which is marketing the product in these countries; so we face no problems in exports.

How many titles do you select in a year?

We select 2 to 3 titles in a year. Till now we have marketed only 20 titles and out of them 30 to 35 percent are on the active list even now. We have sold many titles – over 1 million copies, since we started operations. For e.g., *Family Encyclopedia* by Penguin and *Illustrated Dictionary* by DK have sold more than a million copies and are still selling.

What type of study do you conduct before selecting a title?

In all these years we have learnt one thing – to make a product successful it should appeal to the masses and be of good quality. So we ensure that the title is meant for the masses and the quality is excellent. That is why we deal only with a few but standard publishers.

With which publishers are you currently working and what sort of volumes do you initially commit?

We deal with standard publishing houses like Oxford University Press, Penguin Group, DK, Webster, etc., and our minimum commitment is between 50,000 to 100,000 copies initially.

Any such experience when you were not able to meet the expected commitment and how did you handle the situation?

We have never been in such a situation. With a team of more than 3500 door-to-door salesmen, only an average of 10 copies come to each one which is not such a big number. In fact, we are always short of stocks.

What are your views on the impact of globalisation on marketing?

I feel that marketing has become very competitive today. So many players, all using different kinds of strategies which sometimes are a big annoyance to the consumers but it brings much more benefit to the consumers who today are more aware and have a lot of choices. Also there is less possibility of them being cheated. Globalisation at the end of the day has increased consumer awareness, choices, and possibilities.

Marketing is a challenging profession. Any comments?

I think every product and profession is a challenging one. It depends on how creative or imaginative one is in exposing it to the masses. The key to success is being fearless and confident and then give it your best.

What are your plans for the next five years?

Definitely to give thrust to exports and expanding to more countries such as the Far East, Malaysia, Singapore, Gulf and to the African countries. It is our endeavour to provide more choices to our consumers.

Have you thought of publishing or developing your own product?

Not yet.

I noticed that your visiting card does not have your designation on it. Any particular reason?

One of the most unique things about our business is that everyone involved in it from the bottom to the top has started this business from scratch. We still consider ourselves door-to-door salesmen.

Do you have any Guru or role model?

I began my career as a door-to-door salesman and learnt everything from scratch. In my journey so far I have come face to face with all sorts of people – interesting and fascinating as well as indifferent and disinterested. And I have learnt from both kinds, though stories of some of them have remained with me and such people I consider my Gurus and role models.

Any memorable experience you would like to share with us?

Like I mentioned earlier, some stories remain cemented in your memories. This is one of them. During my salesman days, I used to visit a particular gentleman, once a month, who would buy the same book every month. One day out of curiosity I asked him, "What do you do with so many copies of the same title?" He paused for a moment and then opened a bookshelf. Right there, lined in a row were all the copies that he had purchased from me. Not knowing what to say I stared at him to which he said, "I did not have the heart to refuse you. I wanted to encourage you."

What comprises your typical working day?

I reach office around 10.30 am, each day; I make calls to various distributors, around ten of them and have discussions with them regarding their queries and doubts.

Do you find time to read or study?

I love to read about different cultures. I do not get time to read when I am in Delhi so I do my reading while I am travelling.

How would you describe a good book?

A good book is one which is easy to read and go through, interesting in its approach, has lots of elements of surprise and creates curiosity in the mind of the reader.

Your message to all the upcoming marketing and sales persons.

Here I would like to quote the legendary boxer Muhammad Ali, "Champions are not made in gyms; champions are made from something they have deep inside them – a desire, a dream, a vision". They have to have the skill and the will. But the will must be stronger than the skill. My advice to all is, work sincerely, honestly, with integrity and enthusiasm and always remember the best is yet to come!

(Publishing Today, November 2008)

M G ARORA

Chairman
Universal Law Publishing Company (Pvt.) Ltd. and
Head, Universal Book Traders

Success is not a destination but a journey

You are a self-made man and a successful law bookseller how did you start and what was your journey like?

I was born on 8th March 1933 in an agriculturist family in a remote village that is now in Pakistan. I was studying in 8th class when the partition of India took place. Our whole family moved to a refugee camp in Pakistan where all the occupants used to get meal mixed with sand which resulted in the family getting sick. My grandfather died in the camp followed by my father and my sister who also passed away after migration to India within a span of six months. My ailing mother and I moved to Ambala Cantonment where I joined a high school. After matriculation I applied for admission in a college for further studies but in view of my activities associated with the ideology of RSS, I was denied admission in college. I stayed with my elder brother who had also migrated from Pakistan and was engaged in medical practice. In order to avoid financial burden on my elder brother I joined as a part-time trainee working on a lathe machine in a factory engaged in manufacturing scientific instruments and in my spare time I started teaching some primary students to make a living. At the age of 15, I was arrested in Ambala Cantonment for being a member of RSS which was banned by the Government of India but was released because I was underage. To avoid further complications I moved to Allahabad in 1951 and joined as a salesman with Central Law Agency. I toured various states of India and realised the value of books as people showed extraordinary respect to me as a messenger of knowledge.

What motivated you to start your own business?

Being an RSS member I used to attend Shakhas (daily classes) regularly and also participated in various activities and movements started by them; so I couldn't devote myself completely to my job with Central Law Agency. A few times my employers adjusted with me but they could not do so for long. So in 1956 I left the job and moved to Delhi and started my own business from my house with only Rs. 100 as savings in my pocket. I rented a bicycle and began visiting lawyers and law courts selling them books which I took from publishers on short term credit. Later, in the year 1960 I started a bookshop opposite new Tis Hazari Courts in Gokhale Market. So life started and today 58 years have passed and I have never looked back. I believe success is not a destination but a journey, and I am enjoying the journey everyday.

Share your experience as a salesman and as a bookseller?

During my job in Allahabad, while on a tour in Orissa in 1953, I was travelling on a train from Puri to the then newly developed Ganjam district to obtain orders for the law library. It was a day journey and the ticket collector came to check the tickets. Mostly passenger did not have tickets and were paying the fare to the ticket collector who was keeping the money in his pocket. I was perhaps the only one in the compartment with a ticket. He stared at me as if I had done something wrong.

This left an impression on me and I couldn't sleep. During the night with a candle, I wrote a postcard narrating this incident to the then Railway Minister Lal Bahadur Shastri. After a few weeks I returned from the tour and found a letter in response to my postcard from the minister's office asking me to see him when he next visits Allahabad. I immediately wrote back saying that I am a travelling salesman, and so I will not be able to know the date of the minister's visit. One fine morning a police officer came to my house and asked me to accompany him to the minister. I went with him to Lal

Bahadur Shastri who smiled and asked me to sit by his side. He introduced me to all the senior railway officers and others present in the conference room. Then he took out my first postcard and read out the prevailing state of affairs in the railway department. I was really impressed by Shastri Ji's simplicity, sincerity and quick action. What a difference now?

As a bookseller, I came in close contact with a number of judges, scholars, jurists, law officers and advocates of high academic distinction. Sometimes I have gone out of my way to help the customers by procuring rare and out of print titles for them. Due to this I earned a well deserved reputation. Once K R Naraynan then President of India asked me for a book which was out of print. I procured that book from a UK publisher, who sent the same complimentary. I personally rushed to Rashtrapati Bhawan to deliver that book. He asked me how much to pay and I said nothing sir as it has come complimentary. This and many other such instances have really paid me in the long run. I can not live without going to my bookshop daily. I enjoy doing this as I believe a Bookshop is a Temple; Customer, a presiding deity and I the priest to serve and worship. I would love to be known as a modest, humble and straightforward bookseller.

From a successful law bookseller what prompted you to start publishing?

My relationship with my customers and lawyers are friendly. One day my friend H L Kumar, a lawyer came to me and said "Why don't you publish *Delhi Shops and Establishment Act* which I have authored?" I couldn't say no. So with this I started publishing and it became our first book.

In 1995, I promoted a Company "Universal Law Publishing Co. (P) Ltd." for publishing books by eminent authors, judges, advocates of high academic distinction and law teachers. We have also reprinted over 200 best selling titles on law under licence from more than two dozen internationally known publishers of UK, USA, Australia, Malaysia and Netherland with the objective of making these books available at affordable prices for the benefit of students and professionals. I am proud to say that Universal has built-up a well-deserved reputation in the legal world that continues to be reflected in our ever increasing range of publications and a large numbers of Bare Acts, Rules and Statutes.

I learnt that you were arrested during the Emergency? What was your experience in Tihar Jail?

I was arrested many times, first in Ambala Cantonment in 1949 when the RSS was banned and then in Lucknow in 1954 on my taking part in the Go Raksha Andolan. In the years 1974-75, I was actively associated with "Sampoorna Kranti Movement" headed by Loknayak Jai Prakash Narain when Emergency was imposed. So in 1975 I was arrested and sent to Tihar Jail, where I came in close contact with many political leaders, students and political workers who were also arrested at the time. I saw and observed them closely and realised that a majority of people in politics, are in it for monetary gains rather than to serve the society. I also learnt that there is no room for me in politics. I used to spend a lot of time in the jail library. Though I was released on bail I could not attend to my business and family throughout the emergency period of 18 months; as I was hounded by the local police. During this time my school going children looked after the business.

You were the President of DSBPA in 1990-93. Any experiences you would like to share?

I have been active in DSBPA and FPBA for a long time and held many positions in these Associations. I was made the Chairman of Joint Action Committee (JAC) of both the associations to discipline the book trade and make them adhere to the Good Offices Committee (GOC) decisions. The committee was very active and strict to take disciplinary actions against members for violation of rules. Even some senior members of the executive committee were not spared.

Overall the members cooperated with us and we were able to bring discipline in the book trade.

I learnt that you have earned a place in Limca Book of Records. How were you selected for the same?

On completing 50 years in the book trade and service to the legal profession, the Bar Association of India for the first time decided to honour a non-legal person for providing service to the legal profession. They considered me as a supplier of knowledge to the legal profession. I was honoured and a souvenir was released during the function. This was the reason I was included in the Limca Book of Records, 2004 edition. I also received awards: Distinguished Booksellers Award (1997 from FPBA); Excellence in Law Publishing Award (1998 from FIP); Award for Outstanding Contribution to the Book Trade (1999 from FPBA); Lifetime Achievement Award presented to me by FPBA in their 54th AGM 2008. Federation of Indian Publisher organised a special function in 2007. At that occasion a plaque of honour was given to me by Hon'ble Chief Minister of Delhi Sheila Dikshit.

How would you describe a good book?

A good book is the one which should appeal to the reader and whose contents serve the purpose.

How have you distributed the work between yourself and your family?

Not only sons, my daughter-in-laws and my grandson are also contributing to this family business. I have three sons and all have training in retail trade as I consider it a must for success in publishing. This helps in knowing your customers' mind. Pradeep, the eldest, is a law graduate and looks after publishing and editing of books and reprinting of foreign books in India and his wife Neena also takes interest. Sanjeev, a graduate from Delhi University, looks after the marketing and wholesale distribution of our publications and his wife Vibha is an advocate in the High Court and also a member of the Supreme Court Bar Association. Manish, did a doctorate from Harvard Law School, US He is an advocate practising in Delhi High Court and the Supreme Court of India and looks after the acquisition of new authors and liaises with the legal fraternity. He also runs a law institute to train law entrance students and lawyers for judicial service exams and his wife Purnima looks after the management of the institute. My grandson Anubhav, a graduate, and an MBA from Lincon University (UK) looks after the retail business. Though I have no responsibility now, I cannot live without coming to the shop, come what may. I believe that as long as you work you are young, otherwise you are growing old.

You have been dealing with multinationals. Please share your experience in dealing with them.

"Universal" being wholesale distributors have very cordial relations with the foreign publishers and their associates in India. We regularly import various law related books and journals from UK and USA and also stock their books published in India, but I feel concerned about their way of functioning and the impact of 100% FDI in book publishing in India. The study conducted by some booksellers and publishers associations in India show that more and more Indian publishing companies are being taken over by foreign firms. Some leading law publishing companies have lost their independent status during the recent past. The price fixation formula of foreign companies functioning in India is much higher than the Indian publishers, resulting in high price.

You believe a good book is an excellent friend. What do you prefer to read?

I prefer to read autobiographies, biographies of legal professionals, eminent freedom fighters, revolutionaries and people awarded and honoured for their extraordinary achievements. I love reading and have my personal library in my office and even in my car.

How do you manage to look so relaxed?

I am a satisfied and contended person and my motto now is not to work for financial gain alone, I work so that I can continue to work.

Do you have any hobby?

I sing patriotic songs, and love to watch patriotic and historical movies and watch TV serials on Aastha and Sanskar. I also enjoy attending functions related to the legal profession, legal education and book trade.

(Publishing Today, November 2009)

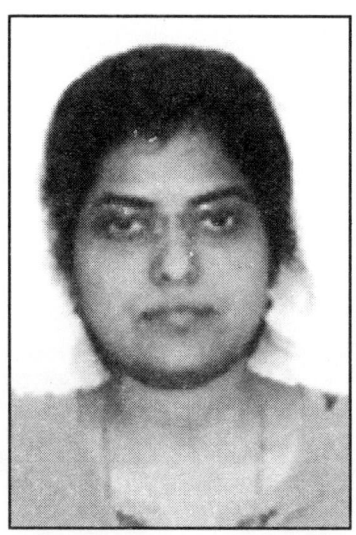

NUZHAT HASSAN
Director
National Book Trust, India

Road to the 'best' is always under construction

Congratulations for organising the 18th New Delhi World Book Fair (NDWBF) professionally and successfully.

Thanks a lot. It was possible only because of the co-operation from the publishers and the participants.

There was a plan to make it a yearly event. Any development?

The plan is very much there and we are working on its modalities.

It is said that international trade buyers visited the book fair in large numbers this time. Do you have any plan to give a boost to this aspect by keeping exclusive trade hours in future?

Not only trade hours, there is a suggestion to have one or two days exclusively for trade visitors and we are looking at these options. Moreover, in order to attract the serious trade visitors to the NDWBF, we have already started many trade-oriented events. For example, this year we had an International Conference titled Professional Publishing in India in collaboration with Frankfurt Book Fair, which was organised on the eve of the Book Fair attended by publishers from India and abroad. Also, our initiative to have an International Rights Exhibition of the Works on and by Mahatma Gandhi drew very good response. I think, such trade-oriented events are a good way of attracting trade visitors to the Fair.

Culturally, Russian participation boosted the image. Do you have any information regarding the trade agreements that they signed during their visit?

As you know, Guest of Honour was a new experience for all of us and this did create a lot of excitement and awareness about the contemporary Russian literature among the Indian readers and publishers. We do hope that with this year being 'Year of Russia in India', there will be more concrete understanding between the publishers of both the countries, especially when the year 2009 will be celebrated in Russia as the 'Year of India'. As far as trade agreements are concerned, generally such information is not shared by the trade with NBT.

Do you believe the best is yet to come in organising the NDWBF and, if so, in which respect?

The road to the 'best' is always under construction; we just need to keep trying to build that sincerely and with a sense of vision.

You organise Children's Book Fair occasionally. Any plans to institutionalise the same in the year when we do not have the World Book Fair?

The concept of Children and Youth Book Fair is a bit different. We have been rotating this in various Indian cities as far as possible.

How many titles did NBT publish in 2007 and in how many languages?

The concrete figure of 2007-08 will come to us in April 2008, but in 2006-07, we published more than 80 original titles and nearly 125 titles in translation in all major Indian languages. If we include the reprints, the figure will cross 900. NBT has been able to bring out books in almost 30 languages, including many minor languages. Further, we have added some new series like Popular Social Science, Indian Diaspora Studies, Afro-Asian Countries Series, etc., under which we are bringing out books to address emerging areas of academic discussion for the general reader.

Tell us something about NBT Book Club and the number of subscribers you have?

Under our Book Club scheme we make lifelong members on the payment of Rs. 50 only. The members get 20% discount on the purchase of NBT books throughout the country. We have more than 40,000 subscribers. The subscribers also receive NBT Newsletters, free of cost.

How many mobile vans do you have and where all do they operate? Do they carry books of private publishers also?

We have 10 vans which go out all across the country down to the panchayat level. Till now, we have covered all districts of India. We had experimented with the concept of carrying books of private publishers also but that was not very successful.

What will be the major thrust areas of NBT in the coming years?

During Golden Jubilee celebrations of NBT in 2007, we had announced many programmes. One of the main thrust areas will be the readership development among the youth of the country for which we are working on a major project, the details of which will be announced in due course. Also, we are emphasising on the publication of original works in Indian languages. Further, our effort to be a facilitator for Indian publishers in terms of enhancement of trade will remain our major priority area.

Are you continuing your hobby of writing short stories now?

I am actively thinking of new ideas which I hope to write very soon.

How would you describe a good book?

A good book is one which holds the interest of the reader and communicates effectively the ideas of the author.

Are you missing your IPS days or enjoying the present assignment?

I am not missing my IPS days but surely enjoying my present assignment as an author and an administrator. I know I have to go back to policing and I am sure this experience will add a deeper dimension to my work.

(Publishing Today, April 2008)

R K MEHRA
Head
Rupa & Co.

Distribution is the key to success

Rupa & Co was set up in 1936 in College Street, Kolkata (then Calcutta) by D Mehra. What is your relationship with him and when did you join the company?

D Mehra was my granduncle; my father, N D Mehra joined him in 1939 and later, I joined the company in 1968 after completing my education. Subsequently in 1970, I moved to Delhi to continue my journey in publishing.

On your move to Delhi, you gave a great boost to the publishing department of the business. Share your experience with us.

I have always been an ardent follower of cricket and back then when I shifted to Delhi from Calcutta, I decided to get into publishing sports books. My experiment began with publishing *Sunny Days* and *Idols* by Sunil Gavaskar, which sold over 1,50,000 copies; this was just a precursor of things to come. This success was followed by books by Vinoo Mankad, E Prasanna, Gary Sobers and Mushtaq Ali. I later co-published Don Bradman's autobiography, *Farewell to Cricket*. These books too sold well, overshooting the print order of a common publisher. Besides sports books, we also published well-known foreign authors like Sidney Sheldon and Jeffrey Archer, which gave the necessary boost to our publishing wing. Apart from having a full fledged publishing list, we are also the only Indian publishing company to have its own distribution network, thereby reaching every nook and corner of the country, and this has contributed immensely to our growth as indigenous publishers. I believe, distribution is the key to success of great publishing.

You publish about 250 new titles every year. What is the size of your workforce?

We have a workforce of around 125 people.

As head of the organisation, what are your responsibilities?

My most crucial responsibility is to provide early growth for the next generation. I make it a point to meet our new and old authors to celebrate our long-lasting relationship. Today Rupa runs like a well-oiled machine, while I get to indulge myself by going to the office 2 to 3 times a week. I now have the time to watch a lot of cricket (I love the game), travel, and read.

Is it difficult finding fiction writers in the face of competition from multinationals?

We prefer to pick up new authors who are acceptable to the Indian readers, unlike most multinationals that are primarily interested in tapping into the Indian market for fulfilling their individual wants. This scenario brings to my mind this quote: "The literature of a society is the mirror of that society."

Tell us about the relationship you share with your authors?

Great! Fantastic! The icing on the cake is that all these authors have become good friends and I enjoy meeting them.

You introduced both Anurag Mathur and Chetan Bhagat. How did you discover them?

We always try to find young authors. This all began in 1991 when I gave a small advertisement stating that we needed authors and since then there has been no looking back. Anurag Mathur and Chetan Bhagat are both very young and extremely talented. We have just published on May 9, Chetan Bhagat's new book, *The 3 Mistakes of my Life* and have already sold 4,00,000 copies. We want to achieve the target of 5,00,000 copies a month. We have also published his two earlier books – *Five Point Someone* and *One Night @ the Call Center* – he is our bestselling author.

You are the pillar of Indian trade publishing. What sort of an action plan do you follow to counter multinational competition?

We strive to do better all the time and try to remain focused in our endeavour to achieve our defined goals.

Normally, the trend in developing countries is to first start with distribution and then advance onto becoming a publisher. Tell us about your journey.

Yes it is so, as a strong marketing network inspires you to do publishing. Earlier we were importing a number of British and American publishers but they willingly began to give the re-print rights to us because of our strong marketing network.

Do you think a publisher should have his own printing unit?

This decision depends entirely on the individual publisher.

Share with us the story behind the logo of Rupa & Co.

Oh, that's an interesting story! My granduncle went to see a play in Calcutta. This play had two characters – Rupa and Son He liked the character Rupa and decided to name the company after it. The logo was designed by noted film director, Satyajit Ray; this was a symbol of his love for us.

What is the percentage of your export sales to domestic sales?

We are very strong in the domestic market; that is, 80% of the sales are within India with 20% being exported.

Do you consider the sale of subsidiary rights important, and how do you promote them?

Yes, it is very important and publishers come to us after seeing the visibility and the sale of our books.

Any plans to go public?

Not at the moment but may consider in the future.

Are you planning to get into e-publishing?

Yes, we wish to.

What are your future plans for the growth of Rupa & Co?

We envisage a growth of 20% year by year, and we will continue vigorously in all our business efforts.

What role does Kapish play in the organisation?

Kapish was completely bitten by the publishing bug and expressed his desire to join the organisation after completing his graduation. He seems to have a talent for spotting bestsellers. The success of Kishore Biyani's book, *It Happened in India* and Chetan Bhagat's success, to a large extent, can be attributed to him.

Does Mrs Mehra help you with the business?

Yes, she is a part of Rupa & Co.

How would you describe a good book?

Any book, which is liked by the reader, becomes a good book.

(Publishing Today, June 2008)

RAJIV BERI
Managing Director
Macmillan India Ltd.

Contribute towards the upliftment of education

Share with us your journey as MD of Macmillan India. Did you achieve desirable results on account of the changes/initiatives taken by you?

It has been a very exciting journey. When I took over as Managing Director in 1995, the company sales were only around Rs 18 crores and now we expect around Rs 260 crores in 2008. The staff was around 800 and now we have 3500 employees. We have been one of the two publicly listed and traded publishing companies and leading a listed company has its own challenges and excitement. We are the only publishing company to be selected as a Business Superbrand, by the Superbrand Council of India. We now publish 300 titles annually and with the Frank Bros acquisition (the first of its kind in India) we now have a substantial market share in the Indian market. We also were pioneers in on-line learning and launched two educational portals in 2000.

Macmillan has been the pioneer in providing BPO services in India. How has this helped you in receiving the Highest Export Award in the Books and Publications Panel?

We have been winning the top Capexil award in our category for over 20 years. The majority of our exports are in the BPO sector and we are exporting digital files. In fact, we are the pioneers in providing BPO services since 1973 and initially were working only for Macmillan International. Word about our quality spread and at present we are providing only 25 percent services to our parent group and 75 percent to other international publishers worldwide.

You have been in publishing since 1976. What prompted you to choose publishing as a career?

I appeared for the IAS exams in 1976 and was waiting for the results when I was approached if I was interested in a job in Tata Mc-Graw Hill (TMH). Without pondering too much over it, I appeared for the interview and was selected. In the meantime my IAS results were declared and I had cleared the exam. Though my parents were of the opinion that I should join the IAS, I personally felt that publishing was a more challenging field. I also felt that India was a highly potential market. I joined TMH and worked there for 11 years. Following various promotions I was working as the Publishing Manager when I left to join Macmillan. I enjoyed my tenure in TMH and had the privilege to work with the best people of the publishing industry. In 1987 I moved on to become the Publishing Director of Macmillan and became a part of the board of directors.

What is the market share of Macmillan in educational books up to the school level?

We publish educational books from classes K-12 and enjoy 17 percent of the market share in the private CBSE/ICSE school market and 22 percent of the English language teaching market in India.

How did the acquisition of Frank Brothers help Macmillan in increasing its market share in the educational books segment?

Frank Brothers at the time of acquisition enjoyed a major market share of top-selling science and mathematics books and also had leading texts for classes 9 to 12. We were relatively weak in these areas and thus the acquisition was a perfect fit and has now placed us in an overall strong position. Are you providing educational publishing on the web as are some other publishers?

As I had mentioned we were pioneers in on-line publishing. Our portal, develop.emacmillan.com provides web based Management Development Programs to corporates, and we have tie-ups with IIM Kolkata, MDI Gurgaon, IIT Delhi and IIFT Delhi.

Recently there was a merger and demerger in MIL. How has this merger contributed to the company's growth?

In 2005-06 we had acquired two typesetting companies, Charon Tec and ICC. Now we have merged these companies in Macmillan India. Also to give even greater focus to our publishing business, we have demerged it into a separate entity, Macmillan Publishers India Ltd (MPIL). Macmillan Group's aim is to buy off outside shareholding in the publishing entity so as to make it a 100 percent subsidiary of the UK group.

Share with us some of the memorable turning points in Macmillan India's 116 years of existence.

Macmillan made its entry into India in 1892 mainly with the purpose of importing books from UK and publishing Indian authors. We owned the copyright to the complete works of Rabindranath Tagore till it came into the public domain. Macmillan published all literary figures from Tennyson to Yeats. We have been publishing *Nesfield Grammar* for the last 50 years. We acquired Charon Tec — a book typesetting company in Chennai in 2005, ICC — a US-owned book setting company in Delhi in 2006, and Frank Bros in December 2006. We set up a new company named MPS Technologies which develops electronic publishing software tools and also provides a digital content platform called BookStore. We have been rated as a Superbrand, we have created substantial wealth for our shareholders, have rewarded them with high dividends, and have created valuable assets in the country.

Is Macmillan International a part of a larger group or is it run independently?

Earlier Macmillan was owned and run independently by the Macmillan family who finally sold it around 10 years back to Holtzbrinck, Germany — a large publisher of newspapers in Germany, and one of the biggest publishers in every area of publishing, be it STM, fiction or digital, academic and educational.

What are your views on electronic publishing? How is it catching up in India?

E-publishing will develop as a support to mainstream publishing and this is already happening. When broadband connectivity becomes universally available and cheaper, e-publishing will get a boost in India; who knows it may grow by leaps and bounds just like the communication industry which has grown in the recent years.

You publish educational books, self-help books, reference books, academic books and journals. Have you introduced any variations in their presentation to avoid piracy and how are you managing this nuisance?

We cannot do very much. We can only take steps to curtail piracy by bringing out new editions at regular intervals and conducting raids as a deterrent. It cannot be avoided totally.

What do you think has been the impact of globalisation on the Indian publishing industry?

The major impact of globalisation has been on digital publishing and web-based learning. Once internet bandwidth becomes much cheaper there will be a revolution in digital publishing. Its affordability will enable all to avail the benefits of distance and digital learning including the common man.

Which will be the focus areas of Macmillan in the next five years?

Our thrust will be in digital publishing, presenting more innovative school books, becoming the number one publisher for management books and to try and contribute in improving the study materials available at the state level.

How has Macmillan been affected by the recent financial meltdown?

I don't see much impact on our domestic publishing business.

Have you published/commissioned the history of Macmillan since its inception in India?

Not yet but have plans to do so.

Share with us how Macmillan India is meeting its Corporate Social Responsibility.

We entered into an agreement with UNICEF in 2003 for a period of five years to develop and print a series of MEENA books. The focus of this was to empower the girl child in rural India. We published and distributed these books (in ten Indian languages) to all the anganwadis throughout the country. More than 50 lakh copies were published on a no-profit basis.

As the managing director what role do you play in the organisation?

Of a visionary, leader, motivator, growth catalyst, and one who charts the direction and path of the company, and evolves a culture in which the employees thrive.

Do you get time to read?

Not really. I travel for almost 10–15 days a month and all my reading happens on flights.

How would you describe a good book?

A good book is one which meets its purpose, makes the reader feel it is worth the money spent on it and leaves a lasting impression on the reader's mind.

(Publishing Today, December 2008)

PADMA SHRI RITU MENON

Managing Director
Women Unlimited

A good book endures, the way you think

Congratulations to you on being awarded the Padma Shri Award - an honour and recognition of the continued efforts that you have put in towards the cause of gender studies and publishing

How did you feel on getting the news about the award?

I never expected it, but was happy that the cause for which we have been working for the last 27 years has been recognised by the Government of India.

How did you come into publishing?

I did my Masters in Literature from Vassar College, in New York, in 1969. I was looking for an opening, but there were not many options for someone with a literature degree. I joined Doubleday, a large trade publisher in New York, the same year, in their market research division. This was one of the happiest accidents in my life because I've remained in publishing ever since!

How did the thought of women's publishing come to you?

I came back to India in 1972 and joined Orient Longman, where I worked with Dr Sujit Mukherjee and Raja Rameshwar Rao. I left in 1974 and joined Vikas Publishing House and worked there till 1984. At Vikas I started the feminist imprint, Shakti, in 1982 and we published quite a few titles. Bikram Garewal, our common friend, introduced me to Urvashi Butalia who was then working with Oxford University Press. She later went to London where she worked with Zed Books; and some time in 1983 Bikram told me she was planning to return, to set up a publishing outfit here. I wrote to her to say I was very interested to hear about this, she wrote back saying, that's wonderful, so we decided to leave our jobs and start Kali for Women. Our focus was on women, of course, from a feminist perspective, and our strong links with the women's movement I think contributed to the success of our publishing. We were able to break even in the first 2-3 years. We were also connected to the international women's movement which helped us a lot in marketing our books and copublishing in various countries.

You are known for taking up the cause of women authors, any particular reason?

Well, most research on issues from a feminist perspective was being done by women but was not being given much importance, so we thought we should provide a forum for it, as well as for material from the women's movement. We also commissioned anthologies, multi-author books, translations from different languages biographies, autobiographies, and general interest non-fiction.

When and why did you break up with Urvashi Butalia?

We had worked together for 20 years and during this time we found that our styles of operating were quite different. In 2003 we decided amicably to work independently, with the understanding that we would continue the work of Kali, which we are doing, sometimes even co-publishing under a joint imprint with Kali.

What are the main things you look at in a manuscript before accepting?

The first criterion is that it has to have a gender perspective and analysis. It should also present new research on issues — environment, religion, development, health, media, violence, fundamentalism, and so on – and of course it should be well written and presented.

You are a writer and a publisher. Which role do you enjoy the most?

Very difficult to say, I like both, it's a happy conjunction. One reinforces the other and I think both benefit.

You are successful in marketing subsidiary rights internationally. What is the key?

Well, a couple of things. One is our links with women's movements across the world; this is a network that spreads the word, which is very important; plus an old association with trade and university presses. By now they know what they can expect from us, they are assured of a certain quality. Plus most of what we publish is original research, often path-breaking. That helps, too.

How would you describe a good book?

A good book is one which endures, one that changes the way you think.

What are your views on digital publishing?

It will affect print publishing but not in the near future, at least not in India, in the social sciences and humanities. Maybe in STM it will be more evident, but it's still in its infancy here.

What are your views on globalisation in publishing?

Well, I think globalisation has hampered the growth of independent publishing and bookselling, worldwide, and when the independents are hard-pressed then midlist authors feel the crunch. It's not good for diversity, what's threatened with globalisation is bibliodiversity, voices on the margins, voices of dissent.

Apart from looking and reading manuscripts, do you read & what is your favourite subject?

I love non-fiction, biographies, travel writing, books of current interest, political trends. And thrillers!

Are you writing any book now?

Yes, I am writing a biography of Nayantara Sahgal.

What makes your day - a big order or a good manuscript?

Reading a piece of writing that is just right.

How do you market your books?

Not well enough, marketing/promotion is always inadequate.

How many new books do you publish in a year?

We publish 12–15 titles (new and reprint) in a year.

What is Maiden Voices?

It is one of our series by adolescent girls but we have published very little so far.

What is the International Alliance of Independent Publishers (AIP) and for how long have you been connected with it?

The AIP was set up in 2002 in France, and has publishers from five language networks – French, Arabic, English, Spanish and Portuguese. The idea is to provide an alternative to multinational corporate publishing, internationally, by disseminating what is published by independent publishers more widely through collaborations and co-publishing projects. The AIP can help with publicity and promotion, and with small grants. Its aim is to work for an alternate globalisation, one of independent publishing.

(Publishing Today, February-March 2011)

S C AGARWAL
CEO
Sultan Chand & Sons

Learning has no age

I organised a one-day publishing seminar for FPBA and there I came to know S C Agarwal. During the introduction, he introduced himself as CEO of Sultan Chand and Sons, educational publisher and throughout the seminar he was sitting quietly but very attentive. At the end of the seminar, S C Sethi President of FPBA asked him what was the secret of his selling books on Cash & Carry and booksellers falling in line to get their books.

He replied that their publications are by very experienced, senior University level professors and low-priced. He said that he was a professor at Ramjas College for 43 years & retired from there in 2004. They first promote their publications with professors & students and then on demand booksellers come and buy on cash. More value less price are the hallmarks of our books. They do not accept any returns or exchange. He also said that they are contributing a part of their profits for the development of education, developing reading habits and giving scholarships to the bright students.

It aroused in me a desire to meet the person who at the age of 71 years is attending a seminar, meeting his social responsibility and quiet enthusiastic about life.

After fixing an appointment I met him in his office and came to know that S. Chand & Company was established in 1917 by Sultan Chandji (1896-1975) who was a pioneer in the field of publishing school and college text books by Indian authors. He had inherited the spirit of nationalism and lofty ideals from his father, Master Amir Chand ji (1869-1915), a dedicated teacher, a social reformer, a great patriot and revolutionary, who was awarded death sentence on 8th May, 1915 for his involvement in the Hardinge Bomb Case.

Now the firm is being run by his daughter Dr Usha Agarwal, a Ph.D in Sanskrit from Delhi University. She taught in various Government Senior Secondary schools as a teacher and principal for 35 years, who never married and retired in 2001. S C Agarwal the youngest son, who has also not married, both (brother and sister team) run the publishing house.

They have established 3 charitable trusts – Shri Sultan Chand Trust (1990), Sri Sultan Chand Dropadi Devi Education Foundation and Dr Usha Agarwal Trust in (2004), under which they give scholarships to the toppers of 1st & 2nd year BCom (Hons.) students of Delhi University, donate books to deserving students, give books for the Book Bank projects. The three trusts have separate abundant Corpus funds of Rs three crore each from which they get abundant interest every year.

The firm has rich heritage of noble ideals for which the Indian Publishing Industry can be proud of and his successors have solemnly pledged to uphold.

They may be among a very few who are not only publishing quality textbooks for the students, but also meeting their social responsibility in a befitting manner.

After my meeting with both the brother & sister team, they presented me a set of inspirational, motivational and spiritual books written by Dr Usha Agarwal, published by the Trust, which are being donated to educational institutions and students regularly.

After the meeting, I felt, if all the publishers start meeting their social obligations, our country will be a different one.

(Publishing Today, December-January 2011)

S K GHAI

Chairman and Managing Director
Sterling Publishers (P) Ltd.
Chairman
Institute of Book Publishing

The world is a book and he who stays at home reads only a page

Congratulations on being elected as the Chairman of the Books, Publications and Printing panel of CAPEXIL. What are your plans for increasing the export of Indian books?

Thank you. Though at this moment it is too early to discuss export plans, however, I do feel that the government should revive the MDA grants to the publishers for their individual-cum-sales study tours. CAPEXIL should organise buyers and sellers meets panelwise so that the meetings should result in business.

Tell us about your decision to enter publishing? Was it impulsive or was it a well-considered one?

After schooling, I wanted to head for engineering but for that I was required to go out of town. My mother prevailed upon me and I joined BSc at D A V College, Jalandhar (Punjab). During that time my father, O.P Ghai was a partner at University Publishers and so I started working part time at the company as a salesman. After completing graduation I joined the company full time at a salary of Rs 200. This was my first brush with bookselling and publishing. Not only did I start liking the work, I fell in love with it and I have remained in love ever since.

How and when did you start Sterling Publishers?

Sterling Publishers was incorporated on 24 November 1964 when I was still in my final year of college; in fact, one of my friend's father helped me to get the company incorporated by spending a mere sum of Rs 679 as the registration fee.

Though I had joined University Publishers, I spent my evenings and early mornings working towards getting Sterling up and running. After 6 months, I left University Publishers and concentrated all my efforts to put Sterling on rails.

You successfully built up a colossal publishing empire with an impressive list, starting absolutely from scratch which is no mean achievement. Please share with us the secret of your success?

It is the commitment, sincerity and hard work, which have gone a long way in taking Sterling where it is today. When we started, at that time Lal Bahadur Shastri had been elected the Prime Minister of India. B S Gujarati, a librarian, approached me with a collection of editorials on Shastriji, the compilation of which became the first book of Sterling. Surprisingly the book did well and we also went into a couple of reprints.

In 1966 I moved to Delhi and began publishing academic books in social sciences and humanities, mainly PhD thesis. We also started working with USIS under their PL-480 program of providing low-cost reprints of University level textbooks for the Indian market. The market for academic books was and still is mainly colleges, universities, institutions and libraries. As we had to deal with such institutions, the cash flow was slow and erratic. So in 1972 we started Sterling Paperbacks keeping in mind the three Es – entertainment, education and enlightenment.

You market your books and give subsidiary rights globally. How do you manage to do it?

We participate in International Book Fairs – Frankfurt, London, Bologna and many others and I also make marketing trips to various countries. I love travelling as it gives me an opportunity to meet with new and different people. I firmly believe that "The world is a book and he who stays at home reads only a page." Working with this in mind, I have been able to develop our export business and marketing of subsidiary rights.

How would you describe a good book?

I believe a good book is one which can be shared with somebody. What better way to share a book than to gift it. A good book is the best gift for all occasions. Though the trend is to send cards, but a book has a life of its own and one can imagine the life of a card.

Since its first issue in October 1969, Indian Book Industry made remarkable progress and became the only respectable professional journal of the Indian publishing industry. We no longer hear of it now. Why?

Indian Book Industry was a vision of my father, late O P Ghai, an individual who placed publishing before the publishers. He believed that for professional knowledge to be useful it was required to be spread far and wide. During that time, no serious professional journal was available in the market except for the Indian Publishers and Booksellers published by the Bhaktals. Indian Book Industry became the only professional journal in the country catering to the needs of the publishing industry. It was quite a tedious job to bring out an issue monthly, so the responsibility of bringing out the Indian Book Industry was handed over to FIP in 1990 as at that time they wanted to start a new trade journal. But sadly only one issue was brought out and after that it was discontinued. Since then no trade journal has come up except journals on book reviews, like Biblio, The Book Review.

What is really sad is that such a huge industry consisting of thousands of publishers do not have a single serious journal to address its common issues.

The Institute of Book Publishing established by O P Ghai in 1985 has been providing training by organising courses and seminars for the benefit of publishing professionals. You have carried forward this legacy with enviable success. What vision do you have for the Institute with the ongoing technological advances in the publishing industry?

A festschrift volume *Indian Publishing since Independence* was published in honour of my father on his 60th birthday. The book was edited by D N Malhotra and Narendra Kumar. During its release, my father said, "What I am today is due to publishing; henceforth I will contribute in bringing professionalism to publishing." This is how the Institute of Book Publishing was born. He started a 1-year PG Diploma course in book publishing and ran this course for one year with only five students. But this course did not draw much attention, so he re-introduced it as a Condensed Course for Publishing Professionals in 1986 and presently I am carrying forward the legacy. We get participants from our neighbouring countries, from Africa and the Middle East, and now from Europe too. The 21st Condensed Course will be held from November 10-19 this year. I feel it is my humble tribute to my father in continuing to organise such courses. Moreover, this helps me to keep myself updated with the latest developments in the publishing field.

When and why did you launch the e-journal Publishing Today?

After the 19th Condensed Course for Publishing Professionals concluded in November 2006, I felt that there was a need to get more actively involved with the publishing fraternity. After discussing the idea with friends in the industry, I launched the first issue of Publishing Today in December 2006. Since then I have made it a point to see that each issue carries an interview of a publishing professional and news about the publishing industry both national as well as international. During the 18th New Delhi World Book Fair this year, I presented the book, *One to One: Glimpses of Indian Publishing Industry* which is a compilation of all the interviews that had appeared in the ejournal since its commencement.

Where do you see Sterling five years from now?

We would like to make Sterling a leading Indian publisher and we plan to consolidate and make our manufacturing unit a world class one, so as to be at par with the global competition.

You are an author, an educator, a publisher and a printer. How do you manage all these by yourself?

For me these are passions and one always has enough time for one's passion. I enjoy working and now my sons – Vikas and Gaurav assist me. Vikas looks after the printing and Gaurav looks after the day-to-day running and the children's publishing program. This way I now have six hands and we are all working together towards a common goal; also this way I am able to take time out for my writing and for the Institute.

What effect do you think will globalisation have on indigenous publishing in India?

Positive, I think. Globalisation will keep us abreast with new developments in technologies and enable us to compete with the big players of the publishing world. It will open up new avenues and markets for exports and the sale of rights. It will improve our production standards and marketing strategies. I am sure that with the vast educational base and the large number of potential buyers, India will definitely be a force to reckon with; all we need is to accept the challenge and organise ourselves methodically.

In this age of information explosion the problem of protection of intellectual property and copyright assumes great importance. As Chairman, Copyright Council of the FIP, do you think that publishers should have their own additional arrangements to check and curb piracy and copyright violations?

With amendments in the copyright laws, India has become very strict in this regard. We have to bring this point to the notice of our authors and also educate our editors that if they come across an uneven style of writing, they should check its authenticity on the internet; so as to eliminate the possibility of piracy. We have to organise more seminars and workshops for the awareness of copyright laws.

How do you visualise the Indian publishing industry five years from now?

The Indian Publishing industry is passing through a golden era. There is a saying in marketing: 'What is seen, sells.' Prior to the Indian markets opening up, the exposure to books was minimal. Books were seen only in bookshops, which were few and far between. The retail revolution in the country has opened new vistas with books being available everywhere. These days, bookshops are not the only place where books are sold. Retail revolution has provided extraordinary opportunities with the opening up of multiplexes, shopping malls and large retail stores which has given a new lease of life to the marketing of books.

How would you describe your journey so far?

I have spent 44 years of my life in publishing and can say with all humility that I have enjoyed every moment of it. It is with the help of the blessings of Shirdi Sai Baba that I am making my vision of publishing come true.

Interview taken by Professor G S Jolly
(Publishing Today, September 2008)

SANIYASNAIN KHAN
Head
Goodword Books (Pvt.) Ltd.

Writing is the byproduct of reading

You are a leading publisher of high quality Islamic books for adults and children. How and when did you come into publishing?

In 1976, my father, Maulana Wahiduddin Khan, started a magazine, entitled *Al-Risala*; At that time I was in the tenth class. I used to go to Chawri Bazar to buy paper and would also visit the printers in the Jama Masjid area quite often. Somehow these visits influenced my choice of making publishing a full time career, which I did in 1983. In 1996 I founded Goodword Books. From 1983 to 1996, I was engaged in publishing books written mainly by my father in Urdu and English.

Did you start the publishing house primarily for your father's books?

The aim was to print Islamic books which were not only attractively illustrated but which were also of a high quality. As there was a vacuum in this area at that time, I decided to launch Goodword Books.

You are a postgraduate in Arabic from Delhi University and belong to a family of Islamic scholars — father, sister, brother. What attracted you to publishing?

I believe I was inspired by my father's writing, especially his interpretation of Islam in terms of peace and non-violence, communal harmony and mutual understanding. I wanted to spread this message, so I selected publishing as a career.

You publish quality Islamic literature. In the initial stages did you have any difficulty marketing your books? If so, then how did you overcome those difficulties?

I never faced any difficulty as such. People were appreciative of the quality and content of our books. Moreover, the publishing fraternity and book distributors helped me to market the books in India and abroad.

You started publishing children's books under Goodword Kidz series in 1999. How is it faring and which are your primary markets?

Our primary markets are the US and UK. Our books are well received in this part of the world. Some countries raised objections regarding certain illustrations but that was something very minor. Overall there have been no problems in exporting these books. I did expect Saudi Arabia to have issues with the books, but instead, objections came from Egypt, where they continue to be raised.

Your mission is to educate the new generation about the real Islamic values. How are you trying to achieve this goal?

I write stories on Islamic subjects and basically they are from the Quran. Every story that I write has a message and a moral value at the end of it. If we can familiarise the younger generation with these values they will grow up as peaceful members of society.

Your books are somewhat high priced. Do you face any difficulty in marketing them?

Yes, I do face some difficulty in marketing my books in India and Pakistan, as these are price-sensitive markets. No such problem exists in other countries.

How far have you been successful in reaching out to non-Muslims in explaining what Islam is?

Reaching out to non-Muslims is our main goal. We regularly organize lectures on interfaith harmony. We attend various conferences in India and abroad and help in spreading the spiritual and peaceful aspect of Islam.

Do you participate in international trade book fairs?

We do participate in some fairs in the international market – Cape Town, London, Frankfurt, Sharjah, Abu Dhabi – and also take part in around 10 major book fairs in Indian cities throughout the year. We market the Holy Quran in Hindi and English at a special price of 20 rupees, which has attracted a lot of attention and has helped in explaining to non-Muslims the real message of the Quran.

Do you give rights of your books to other Islamic publishers or do you prefer to sell your own editions?

We give rights to publishers in other languages, namely Dutch, Malay, Urdu, Uzbek, Turkish, and Bangla, and prefer to market our English edition ourselves.

How do you find the time to write regularly?

Writing is a junoon, a passion, and for your passion you always have abundant time.

Do other members of your family help you with your business?

Yes, my sister Dr Farida Khanam helps me in the editorial and my daughter Sadia Khan helps me in the designing work. Apart from that we have a good team of volunteers who help me with various other jobs.

What makes your day — a good thought or a good order?

Both are needed for making my day. The best day is when a new book comes out and I feel thrilled and thankful when it is well received.

What are the kinds of books you like to read?

Basically non-fiction, which gives me food for thought. Writing is the byproduct of reading. When you read only then will you write.

How would you describe a good book?

A good book should inspire the reader, which for me is the most important element. Also a good book in my case should bring me closer to God. It could be on any subject. For example, after reading Stephen Hawking's *A Brief History of Time*, I was in awe and admiration of the manner in which God had created our huge universe. If creation itself is so big, then how big is its Creator?

(Publishing Today, August 2008)

SAUGATA MUKHERJEE
Publisher
Pan Macmillan and Picador India

Publisher should be professional and open to change

What made you join Harper Collins as a copy editor while doing MA MPhil in 2000?

While I was studying for my MPhil in JNU, I got an offer from both a newspaper and Harper Collins (HC) for a copy editor's job. I decided to join a publishing house (HC). I was excited that I was going to work with books and be paid for reading them! My entry to publishing was not planned at all — it was sheer chance that I came into publishing.

Share your experience at Harper Collins.

I joined as a Copy Editor, at the junior most level in the editorial department. But it was an enriching experience. Worked with some great authors, also got a chance to go through the slushpile — something most newcomers into the industry need to do! There was so much to do. I had my hands full with copyediting but also started getting a chance to talk about commissioning titles. It was a great learning curve for me. My first boss, Renuka Chatterjee, was very supportive.

How did you get an offer from A M Heath & Co. UK?

After my stint at HC, I had gone back to academics, but always kept a slim publishing window open. I had applied to A M Heath — all of this happened because an author friend of mine in the UK asked me to apply for the position. I did so with her encouragement, and it worked! Heath appointed me as an Associate Agent.

Your memorable experiences at A M Heath & Co.

I got an offer to work in UK which I accepted. Here I was reading, assessing the manuscripts and recommending them for publication. It was a boom time for writers from South Asia – it was the post *God of Small Things* era. I got an opportunity to assess a number of proposals from South Asian writers, which widened my outlook and gave me a sharp eye to catch the right proposal. I read known and unknown authors which helped me in knowing the current trends as well. Here I was approached by R K Mehra, my earlier boss at HC, to join him in Rupa as an acquisitions editor to which I agreed and came back to a publishing house.

You have worked with Publishers and Literary Agents, who do you like better?

Definitely with a publisher, which is possibly why I have spent more time there! Also in a publishing house one can go through the entire cycle of acquiring a book to actually publishing it and making it work in the market – which is greatly exciting. In a literary agency the focus is more on finding the right place for the book – I think the responsibility is lesser in many ways though the relationship with the author and keeping it intact takes up a major share of work there. Frankly, the challenges in a publishing house and in a literary agency are quite different.

Your memorable catch at Rupa as an acquisitions editor?

At Rupa my boss was R K Mehra and I enjoyed working with him. In fact while I was working with A M Heath, he invited me to work at Rupa I did lots of acquisitions for Rupa during that period. Ramesh Menon's *Mahabharata* was an exciting project that I acquired and edited. It is in two volumes, fast selling, expensive and I believe is being reprinted time and again. I think it is a permanent/everlasting book and will continue to sell for a long time despite being bulky and pricey.

Do you enjoy working day in day out with authors?

Yes, it gives me an opportunity to liaise with creative minds, develop healthy relationships, mutually beneficial to both sides and it also widens my horizon as a publisher.

How was your second term at HC?

HC was quite small when I joined, but in the 5 years I worked there, it grew at a phenomenal pace to become the second biggest trade publisher in the country. Personally, it was a hugely satisfying stint – I commissioned and published many books and was supported all through by my bosses V K Karthika and P M Sukumar. It was good to grow with a company that was eager to prove itself. It was also deeply satisfying to see so many of my books doing well in the market.

With which well known authors have you worked and your experience?

Worked with many authors in my stint at HC and I think it'd be unfair to mention just a handful of them. I had great rapport with all of them and I continue to work with some of them even as I set up a new list for Pan Macmillan India.

Which has been your most satisfying professional relationship?

In publishing most of your professional relationships actually turn out differently – they become quite close and dear friends. Most of my authors are very good friends with me and I cherish the relationship I have with them. I think it's only fair to say that all relationships I have developed over the years in publishing are very satisfying.

I understand, if correctly, that Macmillan is an umbrella organisation for the group and other imprints work independently.

Right! Macmillan is an umbrella organisation and Pan Macmillan (PM) comes under that. Earlier we were mainly distributing the UK list in India and publishing very few books under Picador (all of which was commissioned in the UK), but now we are a new company - Pan Macmillan India – where we will not only distribute Pan Macmillan UK titles but develop our own original list. We will be publishing under three imprints - Pan, Macmillan and Picador. In Pan we will develop commercial, mass-market fast-moving paperbacks, Macmillan - trade non-fiction, business books and in Picador - literary fiction and non-fiction.

PM works in 70 countries with 41 offices. How does it collaborate?

Every year in Frankfurt we have a meeting of group publishers which is chaired by Stefan von Holtzbrinck, owner of the Holtzbrinck Group of which Macmillan is a part. Here all the publishers of their imprints from the world over give a presentation of their forthcoming highlights which unite the group and we are able to develop personal relationships among ourselves.

You are a multilingual MNC and you can sell rights between yourself. Does this happen or you look outside?

We look outside and between ourselves also. As you know very well not all books work in all territories, so one needs to be flexible in approach.

How would you describe a good book?

A good book is original in thought, plot and structure and makes you curious to read more. It needs to be readable on one hand and original on the other.

Your views on globalisation and its impact on Indian publishing?

We can't run away from it. It is here. We can't sit on our laurels and should adapt to the changes, more so now than ever before. We should become more professional, be a part of the change that is imminent rather than be resistant to it.

Do you think print publishing will die or perish with the onslaught of digital publishing in the next five years?

Printed book is never going to perish. The digital book may outnumber the printed book in sales as its reach is more and is directly proportional with internet penetration. It is indeed easy to procure without moving out from your place. No wastage of commuting time and is available 24x7. No large or prominently located physical place needed, avoiding huge market rents.

What is your opinion regarding royalties on printed book verses digital book.

There should be more royalty on a digital book rather than on a printed book and it should be on a net receipt. It's only natural that the royalties should be more in digital books than printed ones primarily because of the medium in which it is published.

What are your hobbies?

I run in the morning. I like listening to Hindustani classical music and am also a great fan of world music. I also love playing with my son, who has turned three years old. Playing with Vivaan is a great stress buster! Also I read out to him – I have read more kids books than ever before in the last couple of years!

What are your views on the copyright amendments for which the bill is under consideration in the Parliament?

Absolutely rubbish. This will encourage India to be the dumping ground of the west. Moreover, publishers will not give rights to Indian publishers for the latest editions fearing that the territories restrictions will not be honoured.

You have won many honours/fellowships/awards. Which one has been dear to your heart?

I was awarded Paul Hamlyn fellowship for Publishing Executive and was chosen for the Jerusalem International Fellowship Programme 2007. I was also awarded the Frankfurt Editorial Fellowship 2007.

I was surprised when I received an email that I have been chosen in the VIP programme of publishers organised by the

Australian Arts Council, one can't apply for this fellowship; one needs to be chosen by the Arts Council. I was invited to Sydney Writers Festival in 2009. There I learnt that I was the youngest VIP to be selected. It gave me an opportunity to network and make friends with international writers and industry professionals.

How would you rate the social responsibility of a publisher?

It is a big responsibility that publishers shoulder. And I too believe in publishing socially relevant works. We need to be careful about what we publish, because the written word has a lot of import. While publishing is all about being creative and allowing new voices to be heard, one needs to be careful too about the content that goes into print.

(Publishing Today, July-November 2011)

SHYAM DESHPANDE
Head
Rajhans Publications

Publishing is a social responsibility

What made you switch over from teaching to publishing?

I had decided right in the beginning that I would have a career in writing and publishing. I have been writing since I was a kid. I wrote a diary when I was in the fifth grade. It was published in 2001 the way I had written it. It was called *Vahitale Balpan* (Childhood in a Notebook). I also wrote short stories and plays while in school and also the biography of Lord Bedan Powell. When I was in the eighth grade, I won a medal at the hands of Dr S Radhakrishnan. I got an opportunity to be a part of the international scout-guide jamboree in Canada when I had just passed my tenth grade. A boy from an obscure village travelled to 10 countries! I penned the experiences that I had on this trip. The draft was ready by 1970-71 but I couldn't find a publisher for it. Some even asked for money. It was then that I thought of starting my own publishing venture. My wife was also an academician and because she was very supportive, I could leave my job at 29 and start Dhara Prakashan and later Saket Prakashan from Aurangabad.

In those days, most of the Marathi publishing was carried on either out of Pune or Mumbai. At such a time I started off this enterprise in Aurangabad which was then not the most ideal place in terms of being conveniently located. I did it out of a sense of responsibility and with all faith. I didn't have much to invest in the business. My family hailed from a small village. I had neither the financial support nor the requisite educational background when it came to my family. We ran the house on my wife's salary and invested whatever I earned into publishing. My wife did that for a while after which she too left her job when the business expanded. Later, she started taking care of the administration and accounts of the publishing house. I was on the move, busy with the marketing of the books as also travelling and writing. I returned home only on weekends. I was trying to balance my writing as well as publishing. The reason behind my wish to involve myself full time in publishing was my love for books since I was a kid.

I was introduced to good reading while in school. After my schooling I lived in Aurangabad for further studies and that's where the Govt. regional library opened a treasure-trove of books to me. It was then that I made up my mind to work with books.

You're a well-known writer yourself. Many of your own books have been published and you have handled many genres of writing. Your books have also won many awards from the State Government of Maharashtra and the Government of India as also other literary bodies. Did you become a publisher because you are a writer at heart?

I passed out of school with very good marks. Forty years ago, kids who scored that well opted either for medicine or engineering. I decided to pursue my BA in Arts. One of the professors then suggested that I choose the science stream. I told him politely, "I want to be a writer and start my own publishing house." Writing was my breath and when I got the opportunity, I started working towards being a publisher.

What are the kinds of books that you publish?

I started publishing 34 years ago. For a couple of years I focused on novels, short stories, plays, and travelogues as also literary criticism. I was always on the lookout for new subjects and promising writers. I'm happy to say that 60 per cent of the books that I published in the first 10 years were by new writers. There are a lot of well known writers today whose first books were published by me.

In the second and third decade of its existence, Saket Prakashan started publishing a wide spectrum of books. Along with purely literary works, we also started looking at books pertaining to agriculture, ecology, science, sports, travel, health, diet, beauty, yoga, personality development, education, hobby, biographies, works of J Krishnamurthi and Osho and also children's literature which is very rich. My publishing house had brought out 1,400 books so far.

Can you talk of a project which has been truly special for you?

Our country had been ranked high in terms of population and illiteracy. It was a huge task for the Government to ensure basic reading and writing skills in people. It was the responsibility of the Government to bring out books that were written specifically keeping in mind the neo-literate populace. Unfortunately, the way it was done by the Government was marked by its predictability and mundane nature. At this time, individual publishers could have roped in experts and brought out literature specifically for the neo-literate. Hardly anyone did that but Saket Prakashan brought forth suitable literature which was much superior in its thought, content and treatment than the Government projects. In those days there used to be Government competitions for the writings published in this niche. One hundred and five books won awards out of which 75 were brought out by Saket Prakashan. We started *Shabdasangat*, the first bulletin for the neo-literate for the National Literacy Mission. It went on for 10 years. I'm happy that we were involved in such an important project on a national scale.

What has been your experience of writers? Can you share an anecdote with us?

A writer is the spine of a publishing house. It is the writers that make a publisher proud. No publishing house can run on its own. There are a lot of forces at work which support and encourage its growth and success. The three rules of this industry are to protect the writer's freedom, ensure his rights and to compensate him justly. I've been a fortunate man. Because I was a writer before turning into a publisher, I knew what the writers had to go through. I wouldn't want anyone else to go through something similar. At times, we might miss out on something but the best thing in such a case is to rectify the mistake. The last 34 years have given me some wonderful memories. They gave me the strength to carry on. As for those memories that were less-than-wonderful, I have wiped them off.

Globalisation has seen a lot of publishers in English entering Marathi publishing. Do you look at it as a challenge or competition?

Today, one has to face challenges brought by globalisation in every industry. The English publishers entering Marathi publishing is a fallout of this and we must welcome it as a natural process. Instead of looking at it as competition, Marathi publishers should look at it as an opportunity to exhibit their own high standards and ingenuity. It's a healthy competition. Each one has to survive using the best of his abilities. You have to look at the situation positively and optimistically.

What is the nature of Marathi publishing and how would you like it to be?

Very often, Marathi publishing is a one-man show. There are very few publishing houses where the third generation is carrying it forward. Publishing houses have different departments for editing, production and marketing. Barring a few honourable names, very few publishers take it seriously. Publishing is a social responsibility. It's not only business. It's also a cultural responsibility. It's essential to have some basic qualifications to be a part of it. Doctors and engineers need to be qualified to do their job, but just about anyone can become a publisher. It's an unfortunate reality of today. Some people with zero knowledge or understanding of literature, writing and distribution have entered this trade and this hasn't been too good for it.

Your children are in this business too. How do they help you?

My daughter Dhara worked with me till she got married. She herself is a good writer and it really helped us. My son is a creative photographer and is qualified in marketing. After I crossed 50, more than eight years ago, I left the responsibility of the publishing house to him. My daughter-in-law is an MBA and she too is active in exploring newer horizons according to the changing tastes of the readers.

I'm happy at the way things have shaped up in the past eight to nine years thanks to my son and his wife, Pratima. They have moved with the times and are happy with the response that they have got from the readers. It encourages them. This year we have an ambitious project. We are going to bring out the translations of works of seven Nobel Prize winning writers. We have also started on some more Marathi translations of the works of the big names in world literature.

In conclusion, would you describe yourself as being a happy man?

I worked on a couple of small businesses before I started publishing. I also made good money in some of them but my heart was not in it. I came home to publishing. At times, there were other opportunities/ temptations, which would have been more satisfying monetarily but I turned my back on them because they wouldn't have made me happy. I had always decided that I wouldn't do something that did not give me satisfaction and joy. I stayed put as a publisher. Now the only things that I focus on in life are my writing, reading and being there for my son.

(Publishing Today, September-October 2009)

SRIDHAR BALAN
Publishing Consultant
Ratna Sagar (Pvt.) Ltd.

Publishing is a creative profession

How and when did you come into publishing?

I was an academic prior to joining the publishing industry. Initially, I was a consulting editor to a *Right to Property and Fundamental Rights* book and a 2 volume series on the *Indian Constitution* edited by Justice Hidayatullah and published by Arnold Heinemann. My first regular job in publishing was as a senior editor in Macmillan in 1983. I joined OUP in 1985. I left my formal position as a director in OUP on 1 January 2003 but continued with them as a consultant till the end of 2004.

You were a freelance columnist with the leading newspapers and a professor. What attracted you to publishing? What subject you were taking?

I guess I like both teaching and writing. The teaching job in the Dept. of Political Science at the North-Eastern Hill University in Shillong was both exciting and challenging and I must say I enjoyed those years. I had started contributing academic articles to newspapers even then and started writing regular columns for newspapers after I joined publishing. The only difference was that these were now articles on issues facing the industry.

How did you like the change?

Ironically, if you review the careers of most of the stalwarts in the publishing industry, you would find that most of them 'drifted' into publishing after having started somewhere else. A colleague of mine had once remarked that the best publishers were 'failed' academics. I don't know how good an academic I was, but I hope I have contributed something to publishing.

Which profession did you like the most: Teaching/Columnist/Publisher?

If you like books and reading, I guess you will like publishing. It's a very creative profession calling for diverse skills. At the end of the day, if you hold a well-designed product in your hands that is, at the same time, eminently readable, your satisfaction can be great. The monetary compensation may not be great initially but being in the company of educationists, academics and general authors more than makes up. I certainly look back with satisfaction at the years I spent and continue to spend, in publishing.

You were a Course Director for a 3 months course on Publishing with FPBA. How was the experience?

I enjoyed the 3 month stint as director of the course on publishing at the FPBA in 2003. Actually, my involvement was longer than that, as there were organisational matters to attend to, prior to the course. It was a well-structured course with full academic rigour including periodic tests and assignments. The course was the vision of three stalwarts in the industry, Sukumar Das, then of UBSPD, Dr N Subrhamanyam, then of TMH and K P R Nair of Konark. We had some bright students too who were later absorbed in the industry.

You have written so many articles, why have you not written a book? Are you planning to write one?

All the articles that I have published in books have been commissioned ones and have involved some research. As a columnist in The Hindu, The Economic Times, The Indian Express and The Financial Express (at different times) I was free to write my own pieces, provided I stuck to the word-length! I love contributing to the Biblio (where I am a trustee) because we are a little liberal with the length. No, I have not thought of writing a book because no one has yet asked me.

What is your assignment at Ratna Sagar?

When I joined Ratna Sagar in 2005, my appointment as senior consultant just carried one line "to help Ratna Sagar grow in every way". In the 29 years since its inception, Ratna Sagar has consolidated its position to become one of the leading publishers in India. Growth has helped it to diversify its product range. In addition to its educational books, it now has a distinguished academic imprint, Primus and also some fine medical and health related books in collaboration with Byword Books. We have also taken on a range of dictionaries for exclusive promotion and distribution from HarperCollins. I hope I have played some role in Ratna Sagar's growth.

Do you influence recommendations of textbooks with teachers/professors?

I help to build a positive relationship with Ratna Sagar and its customers, be they educational and academic institutions and the trade. If, in this process, Ratna Sagar increases its business, well and good! I am particularly happy with a program I take on reading in leading schools. There is widespread concern about a decline in the reading habit among children. I hold an interactive session with teachers about how we can redress this and make the world of books come closer to that of children.

What are your views on globalisation in publishing?

Rightly it's said that publishing has not changed as much in the last 200 years as it has in the last 20! The frenetic selling and buying out of companies in the 1970s and 1980s has resulted in much more integration and consolidation now. The publishing company has become one more arm of a multi-billion dollar octopus – a conglomerate. While this has resulted in the greater availability of financial resources for publishing, it has also resulted in books being viewed as revenue generating commodities. The conglomerate's approach to publishing is very different to that of the great publishing gentlemen of yesteryears who established great imprints in their own name. Today, a book is seen as 'a product to be quickly produced, attractively packaged, effectively advertised and completely sold!' Unfortunately, the nature of books is such that they do not easily lend themselves to such an approach. The flip side of globalisation has resulted in India feeling the need to compete in the international market. It has resulted in the industry becoming more professional. We see this in better editing, better layout and design and better finished products. This has helped in better acceptance of our books both in the domestic and foreign markets. India is no longer looked upon as merely a market for imported books, but is an active co-publishing partner with international publishers. Greater technological innovation and inputs have resulted in maturation of the printing industry and resulted in increased export earnings. The publishing industry has played a complimentary role in getting global recognition for Indian writers in English.

What are your hobbies?

As can be guessed, I love reading both fiction and non-fiction. I reserve a part of my weekend for reading and spend at least a couple of hours on this. I also use the books I am reading to illustrate a point or two in my articles. Since I travel on work quite a bit, I find it a great opportunity to catch up on reading. As our home underwent renovation recently and all my books had to be packed off into cartons, I found the occasion to write a piece, 'Books are Memories on Shelves'. While packing my books, I found myself reminiscing about when and where I had got them. One of the most difficult things is to discard books. All of them have given you so much pleasure. I love sports and watch most games on television. In the 1960s, I had seen some memorable cricket and tennis matches live on the ground. Two of them stand out. In the year 1966, Gary Sobers's team from the West Indies gave us an innings defeat, in the Eden Gardens in Kolkata, in 4 days after the crowds rioted and play was abandoned for a day. In 1968, Ramanthan Krishnan made a memorable comeback after being down 2 sets and 2-5 in the third set in the Davis Cup tie against Thomas Koch of Brazil. That memorable win took us to the Challenge Round against Australia.

What is your message to young publishers?

I consider myself as still young, in the sense of learning new things continuously! As far as young publishers are concerned, I think they need to be aware of the changing environment of publishing. While books may still endure, the jury is still out whether the future of reading will still be in the print format or will it become digital. I would like publishers to keep themselves open to publishing in the digital format and see the enormous possibilities of e-publishing. The e-pub format gives you better scope for an ongoing relationship with the reader in the form of reader reviews, discussions with the author, etc. Also, publishers could think of innovative ways in which the e-book could support the promotion of the printed book. Customers would need reading matter to be read on various devices across different platforms. The publisher, being the master of content, would have to provide this.

How would you describe a good book?

A good book can be described as something that should excite the imagination and keep you engrossed. It's not necessary to read the book in one go. Rather, the book should make you ponder, think and sometimes you may like to look up references for what you have read. I have seen many readers marking passages in the book they are reading or scribbling notes in the margins. While I would prefer notes should be made separately, nevertheless I am happy the book has made such an impression on them. We need to do a lot more for books and for the printed word. Reading can be strengthened with both visual and audio support. It's a great experience to read while listening to an audio version of the book. I think appropriate visuals too will greatly enhance reading.

What is the future of a book?

With the advent of the e-book and reading becoming widespread in a digital format either on e-readers and other devices, people have been quick to sound the death knell for the printed book. I think the p-book having endured for so many years, is quite resilient and may well continue for some more years. Ultimately, the consumer is the king and publishers will have to serve content to be read across a range of devices, as per the customer's choice. The print format will have to be thought of as one more device for reading. There is a lot of romance and nostalgia associated with a freshly printed book, holding it, feeling it and even smelling it! Against this, we have to contend with the seductive charms of the i-Pad, the Kindle or the Samsung Galaxy. To each, his own! The saving grace is, that reading continues. A happy marriage would of course be, where the e-book and the p-book complement each other and where one format can be used to promote the other!

(Publishing Today, April-June 2011)

SUKUMAR DAS

Managing Director
NCBA Exports (Pvt.) Ltd.
Managing Director
UBS Publishers Distributors (2001-2008)

Be good to others, they will be good to you

You joined UBS in 1964 and moved on to become its MD in 2001. Describe your journey in the book industry.

It's been a very interesting and fascinating journey. My romance with publishing began in 1964 and has been going strong ever since, though it was a chance encounter. At that time all my efforts were concentrated on preparing for the IAS Civil Services Examination, having completed my Masters in political science. But fate had other things planned for me. One of my professors fixed an interview appointment for me in a newly-started book distribution house. As luck would have it, my candid answers got me selected, and I joined UBS on 2 September 1964. Immediately upon joining, I was packed off on a 51-day tour of South India which included four states. Though I was a novice and had no idea about bookselling, I played it fair and square. The response was very encouraging and I was also successful in obtaining a large order for UBS from one of the dealers. Since then there has been no looking back. From a sales representative to marketing officer, to sales manager, to Delhi branch manager, to export manager, to export director, to additional export director, to additional managing director and then finally in 2001, Mohan Chawla made me the managing director and he himself became the chairman. My understanding of bookselling and my interaction with booksellers took place during my stint as the Delhi branch manager, but my interaction with publishers occurred when I was export manager. Surely it has been an enriching and satisfying journey all through.

You have been chairman, books panel of CAPEXIL since 1992. Tell us about your achievements during these 16 years and what are your plans for the future?

When I joined, I felt that there was a lack of structured trade information which prevented the exporters from exploiting the country's huge export potential. To facilitate accessibility of such information, I started a monthly newsletter which gave countrywise information and statistics. It was not only informative but proved to be commercially beneficial as well. I also took delegations around the world (except CIS and Latin American countries), which enabled us to view the publishing industry from a global perspective. These efforts urged exports to reach the 1000 million mark – a huge leap forward from the meager 330 million earlier.

For things to look up in the future there is an immediate need to bring about professionalism and provide adequate training to industry professionals, as rapid technological developments take place. Also, the marketing of sales rights by Indian publishers needs to be promoted vigorously in the years to come.

You were elected secretary general, Afro Asian Book Council after Asang Machwe's demise in June 1996. How do you plan to take the council to the next stage of development?

Earlier the membership of AABC was open only to publishers and booksellers but now it has been opened to authors, translators and editors too. We have been organising important seminars and are trying to make the council broad based.

From 2001–2003 you were president, FPBA. What were your achievements during this period?

During my presidentship, I organised a three-month training course and later absorbed all the participants in the industry. I also edited a book *The Book Industry in India: Context, Challenge and Strategy.*

How far has UBS gone into digital printing/CD ROM publishing?

We have not yet started digital printing/CD ROM publishing but are certainly making investments in the infrastructure.

What percent of business do you do online?

Not much, very little. Online business is yet to take off.

UBS has seen many ups and downs; how is it going now?

Going very steady; now there is no question of going down – from here the path moves steadily upward ahead.

What are your future plans for UBS?

I plan to retire from UBSPD (August 2008) and hand the reins to Anshul and his team to carry the legacy forward.

What do you think has been the impact of globalisation on Indian Publishing?

Colossal! Globalisation has changed the face of Indian Publishing. India now produces huge quantities of content which has led to the arrival of outsourcing on Indian shores

You shared a wonderful relationship with Late C M Chawla. Any quality of his which left a lasting impact on you?

C M Chawla was a visionary. Every working hour spent with him revealed a different aspect of his dynamic personality. One could never stop learning around him. Of the many gems, some particular qualities of his, which had a deep impact on me, were his sharp memory, his humility and his ability to identify new talent and repose faith in them.

What kind of a relationship do you share with the present generation of Chawlas?

They are very much like my immediate family and we enjoy an excellent relationship.

Any success mantra for young entrepreneurs?

Hard work and honesty in life go a long way, and never give up hope for a bright and better future – where there's life, there's hope! There are no shortcuts to success and no there is no substitute for dedication.

How do you manage to look so relaxed?

Do I ? I guess the secret is that I refuse to carry any tension home. I can switch on and off very quickly. Meditation too helps in destressing and relaxing.

How does being a Rotarian contribute in your everyday living?

It helps tremendously – mentally as well as otherwise. It is my sincere belief that if you are good to others they will be good to you. Also, learn to be humble as you grow and progress in life.

Do you enjoy travelling?

My first love is books and then travelling, which I enjoy a lot. Also my assignments take me around the world a lot.

Any particular type of books that you read?

I read fiction and love to read comparative religion, which gives me immense pleasure and satisfaction.

How would you describe a good book?

A good book is a book which has strong content, is well-produced lookwise, and has wide acceptance.

(Publishing Today, July 2008)

SUNIL MEHTA

Managing Director
Mehta Publishing House

Selling on cash in the best policy

You are known to have revolutionised Marathi publishing. How did you go about it?

My father initiated the business in Kolhapur in 1965 and started a branch in Poona in 1976. I joined the business in 1986. Before I joined, my father Anil Mehta was publishing books in Marathi and he used to offer credit, sometimes unlimited, to booksellers around Maharashtra. On my joining the business as a Commerce graduate my father handed over the reins of the publishing house to me and stationed himself at our ancestral town Kolhapur and continues to direct operations from there.

I studied the total business and took the unfriendly stand of selling books on cash basis to one and all. The immediate effect was the fall in sales from 30 lakhs in 1986 to 20 lakhs by 1991. But here I must confess that my father never interfered in my policy and rather gave me full support. By doing this I also started publishing the bestselling authors that were in demand and which helped me in going ahead. By 1994, our publishing house was back to making 30 lakhs a year sales.

After seeing the success of my system the other Marathi publishers also started following the practice and this really helped revolutionise the Marathi Publishing Business.

How many new titles and reprints do you publish each year?

We publish around 160 new titles of which 90% are translations and 10% are original works in Marathi. Of the new titles, 60% are a work of fiction. We also publish books on well-being, philosophy, religion, self improvement which have also started selling among Marathi people. We publish approximately 300 reprint titles each year with a print run of 2,000-5,000 copies. We have published about 2,000 titles in Marathi by now.

You have been a pioneer in publishing bestsellers in Marathi. How are these received in the market? Which are the bestselling authors you have published?

We took a risk in translating bestsellers in Marathi but we are happy that these books are selling well in Marathi as well. We have published the books of well known authors like Alistair Maclean, John Grisham, Jeffrey Archer, Robin Cook, Mario Puzo and recently *Slumdog Millionaire* by Vikas Swarup and *White Tiger* by Aravinda Adiga.

Our initial endeavours included Ranjit Desai's historical fiction – *Swami, Shrimanyogi* (Shivaji's Biography) and V S Khandekar's *Yayati*. Of these we sell approximately 7,000 copies a year even now and they have become the backbone of the publishing house.

We have also translated Bandula Chandra Ratna from Sri Lanka who was shortlisted for Man Booker Prize in 2000 and Mohammad Qadra from Australia. We have also published the *Chicken Soup Series* in Marathi.

Do any family members help you in publishing? Also, do you find time to indulge in reading for pleasure? If so, when, and which is the last book you read?

My father has been my guide in publishing and still extends full support. I make the preliminary selection and then if he finally gives his consent, only then do I sign an agreement.

As to your other question, I do not find time to read for pleasure. I only read synopses of manuscripts.

How do you rank yourself in Marathi literary publishing?

We are one of the leading publishing houses dealing Marathi literature and are responsible for introducing various new dimensions in Marathi publishing. We have published the works of many renowned authors like Kiran Bedi, Arun Shourie, Nani Palkiwala, Sudha Murthy, and Bangladeshi exiled author Taslima Nasreen. Many other Indian authors have been introduced by us in Marathi. We have also published Dalit literature by Deepa Mahanavar and Daya Pawar.

Incidentally, we were also the first publishers to have brought out children's books in four colour and have 150 titles at present.

You have one of the nicest publishing showrooms and office. From where did you get the idea/inspiration for it?

For this I give credit to my visits to Delhi and Mumbai publishers.

Tell me something about your website and online selling

We are one of the first Marathi publishers to go online for selling purposes. Our website is updated every alternate day. We accept credit cards and we have dedicated customers as well who buy all our books. Our monthly sale on the website is around Rs 15,000-20,000.

Do you also export Marathi books? If so, where?

Not yet, but our books are being exported through other distributors. We are applying for the membership of CAPEXIL and will start our direct export as well.

How do you run your magazine Mehta Marathi Granth Jagat? *What is it's circulation and readership?*

We publish 15,000 copies ever month and it is mailed to various public libraries in Maharashtra. We have 3,000 paid subscribers and the annual subscription of the magazine is Rs 150. We cover Marathi literary news, new releases, interviews with authors and book reviews.

We also publish our catalogue every month.

What is the concept of T Book Club and how is it getting along?

We have 900 members at the moment and they pay Rs 50 annual subscription for membership and they have to buy six of our translated titles at 50% discount every year.

In your opinion, has Sarva Shiksha Abhiyan (SSA) boosted Marathi Language Publishing? If so, how?

Sarva Shiksha Abhiyan has boosted Marathi language publishing in a big way but we are not a part of this. There are many small publishers catering to the demand created by the initiative but they are not publishing good quality books. We are not in the business of supplying books to the government and therefore are in direct contact with the reader.

How many new Marathi language books are being published annually?

Around 3,000 new titles on various subjects are published each year in Marathi.

Do Marathi publishers use ISBN and barcoding? What effect has it had on the business?

Today all Marathi publishers use ISBN. It helps in exports and in supply to United States Information Service as they do not buy any books without an ISBN. They are also introducing barcoding as it helps with the sales at chainstores, especially at Crosswords.

When you visit International Book Fairs what is your agenda?

To meet new publishers who have no knowledge about India and to establish networking with them and buy rights.

What is the impact of globalisation on Marathi language publishing?

Globalisation has certainly improved the production quality of our books. We have been able to introduce new subjects in Marathi, such as Self-help books, and these are now sold in greater numbers. This has boosted their translation and we have been able to develop an efficient team of translators and editors for the purpose.

How do you think shopping mall culture has increased the sale of regional language books?

With this culture the display area of books has increased and regional language books have better sales in the regions they belong to, as well as across the country, thereby boosting their publishing.

It has also affected the work culture, and with that, we learnt to keep our showroom open 7 days a week from Crossword. Also as Crossword is open up to 10 pm we are also planning to prolong our working hours.

The training course started by Poona University with Marathi Prakashak Sangh has closed down. What do you think is the reason?

It was stopped due to red tapism in the University. We met the Vice Chancellor but it was of no use.

How many Marathi Publishers and Booksellers Associations are there? How many publishers are actively engaged in Marathi language publishing and who are these?

We have two Associations – Marathi Prakashan Parishad and Akhil Bharatiya Marathi Prakashak Sangh.

There are 10-15 major publishers in Marathi language; Rajhans, Mauj, Popular, Saket and Majestic, to name a few.

How would you describe a good book?

The book which gives a good message for the society, the reader loves to read it a number of times, where the book is recommended for every book lover and it has content and production values. I think a good book is one which is equally appreciated by readers as well as our editors and critics, despite the subject. It should get a good response from readers, it should drive the attention of critics as compared to contemporary books as well as be a literary landmark.

(Publishing Today, April 2009)

PADMA SHRI TEKKATTE NARAYAN SHANBHAG

Head
Strand Bookstall

From a Bookstall owner to a legendry Bookseller

Tekkatte Narayan Shanbhag, the legendary bookseller, passed away peacefully on the morning of Friday 27th February, 2009 at his Pedder Road residence. He was 85.

Students, authors, academicians, celebrities, opinion makers, publishers and the high and mighty in India, all alike knew him as the BOOKSELLER. The nation rewarded him with the Padma Shri in 2003, not for being an author but for being a one man revolution in bookselling in India.

He was born the son of a rich landlord in a village in south Karnataka in 1925. But his father passed away when he was only two-and-a-half years old. His mother was from a poor family and could barely read Kannada. An uncle who was staying with them as a dependent managed to grab all their property, including his mother's jewellery, and even refused to have him educated.

Undeterred, the young Shanbhag sat for the poor boy's fund examination, stood first and studied with the help of the scholarship. A voracious reader since his childhood, he completed his matriculation, joined St. Xavier's College in Mumbai and took up a part-time job to support himself through college. Such was his passion for books that in those days, he would walk all the way to Tardeo from college to save the Rs 5 monthly tram fare, and buy books instead.

At times he used to visit a big bookstall in Bombay. One day the salesman denied him entry and rudely asked him what he wanted. When he expressed the desire to browse through

Penguin's cheap editions, he was given a disdainful look, and unceremoniously denied.

This offensive incident left a deep impression on Shanbhag and he decided to open a bookshop where people would be allowed to browse unhindered. Then began the arduous two years when he skipped meals, walked instead of taking trams and made many other sacrifices to amass his capital. At the end of it, he began looking for a kiosk with a capital of Rs 450. This was in the late 1940s, when Mumbai had just 12.5 lakh inhabitants, and stretched from Colaba to Boribunder.

He settled for a 'hole in the wall' in Strand Cinema, one of the six theatres that screened English films at that time. In the owner K K Modi, a self-made man, Shanbhag found a willing ear. Modi understood his earnestness and set up a kiosk for him.

On November 20, 1948, he inaugurated the kiosk at Strand. He began with two basic principles, talking to customers and building relationships with them and offering small discounts. Soon, prominent people like Sir Ambalal Sarabhai, the then Bank of India chairman, and the retired Diwan of Mysore, Mirza Ismail became his customers. The first three years were a struggle with a mere Rs 1,200 monthly sale. In the third year, sales rose 10-fold and the business became viable. He got married around this time.

In 1953, V H Gumaste, chief government pleader in the High Court, offered him a place in Fort. Shanbhag's client, Chief Justice M C Chagla, became his guarantor and the Strand Book Stall found its new premises in Fort in November. Around 1960, Shanbhag made his first million. By then his customers included T T Krishnamachari, Y B Chavan and Jawaharlal Nehru.

Shanbhag continued to offer discounts; and made it a point to sell good books at very competitive prices, keeping his margins really low. It was his belief that knowledge like air should be free. In offering discounts, he became the first one to break the anti-reader Net Book Agreement (NBA). He was the only bookseller in the world who offered a 20 per cent discount on published prices to his clients out of 25 per cent available to distributors. The Agreement prevented a bookseller from giving discounts and until then booksellers had not dared defy publishers for fear of stoppage of book supplies.

Shanbhag derived unmitigated pleasure from the experience of watching people come to life in the healing and redeeming presence of books. His children inherited his love for books. His daughter and later on his partner Virkar opened the Strand Book Stall in Bangalore 13 years ago. His son Arun, is the CEO, Rising Book Company in the US.

Shanbhag's literary influence rubbed off on many. His illustrious list of clients included Dr APJ Kalam, a young scientist then, industrialist JRD Tata, writers Khushwant Singh and V S Naipaul. Once Khushwant Singh declared on a BBC show, that Strand was the only 'personal bookshop' in India.

He was known to be in constant touch with Indian and foreign authors enhancing his knowledge on the kind of books he should read, collect and sell. With his huge and varied collection he began the Annual Strand Book Stall Sale, at the spacious Sunderbai Hall in South Mumbai. The venue plays host to thousands of readers for the 20 days of the sale. The sale sees more than 30,000 titles.

Once he told the press in no uncertain terms that "those who say that people do not read anymore are liars, they do not know what they are talking about". His success, he explained, is because he is more of a book reader than a book trader. "I am on the same side of the counter as the reader; I give discounts till it hurts." He views, other booksellers as traders who could just as well be selling shoes. He was a voracious reader and had a personal collection of 6,500 titles, of which he read every single one.

Shanbhag, was honoured with a Padma Shri in 2003. Too little too late, some may say. The intellectual world in India owes a deep debt to him for making available the best books in all disciplines of knowledge at affordable prices. The honour elated him but more so the affection of his innumerable friends from all walks of life all over the world. Shanbhag said, "I am elated, of course. I think my friends Soli Sorabjee, N Narayana Murthy, Azim Premji and others recommended my name for the honour. As you know I have never sought nor wangled for honours in my life," He was, of course, more comfortable with books alone, his lifelong source of divine joy.

Despite the emerging competition, Shanbhag never succumbed to the pressures of the marketplace and refused to stock even a greeting card, let alone a soft toy. He expressed his views to a newspaper, saying, "I firmly believe, as a bookseller, that the moment you divert money into anything other than books, you are insulting *Saraswati*." He found other ways to expand his business and saw the setting up of the website www.strandbookstall.com With the help of the website he hoped to spawn several Strand outlets nationwide. However he did not believe that the internet would ever dispense with the need to 'see and feel' a book prior to purchase.

Shanbhag did not give in to the frills of coffee and music at his bookstore. A booklover himself, he sought to make books affordable and accessible to many who are laymen as he once was. In his ardent pursuit for a warm space that would provide unmetered book browsing privileges, and be commercially viable, he has left an enviable footprint that many will aspire to.

(Publishing Today, March 2009)

VIKAS GUPTA
Managing Director
Wiley India (Pvt.) Ltd.

Books are the only commodity that is cheaper in India

After acquiring an engineering degree in Electronics, what made you pursue publishing as a career option? How did this unique combination come about?

In fact, publishing has been my family business for over three generations. As I was slated to join the family business, my engineering background came in handy, especially in respect of publishing of computer and IT related books. When I began in 1992, the IT business in India was in a nascent stage and there was a growing need of varied IT products. Following this cue, I ventured out to redefine computer publishing and how computer learning could be acquired through books.

In addition to the Bachelor of Electronic Engineering from Pune University (1985), I also acquired a PG Diploma in Printing and Publishing from London College of Printing (1989) and Diploma in Sales and Marketing (1991).

How did Dreamtech Press Pvt Ltd start?

My father and I left the family business in 1999 to start the Dreamtech Press with a small seed capital. At that time I was able to forge a joint venture with an American publisher, IDG Books Worldwide—a company which was later acquired by John Wiley & Sons Inc., US. Around this time, simultaneously, I also started an e-learning software company by the name of Dreamtech Software, whose e-learning platform was acquired by a US Company in early 2001. This deal gave us the capital investment required to meet our financial obligation with our foreign partner in our publishing joint venture.

The joint venture was named as Wiley-Dreamtech Pvt Ltd. However, in 2006 Wiley-Dreamtech became a 100 per cent subsidiary of John Wiley & Sons by the name of Wiley India subsequent to the acquisition of the remaining shares by John Wiley.

How many books have you written and what are your future plans in this respect?

In all I have written 15 books so far, including the best-selling *Comdex* and *Rapidex* series of computer books, which have sold over 2 million copies till date.

I have also co-authored a six-book series on computer science called *Cracking the Code* published by John Wiley and Sons Inc. US In addition, another book co-authored by me has been published by Mc-Graw Hill, US.

Incidentally the Comdex Series continues to be a publishing blockbuster selling more than 1,50,000 copies every year.

I understand that you have been a recipient of different honours and awards individually and for the company from time to time. Can you please elaborate on this?

In 1998 I was nominated for the prestigious Sista World Com Young Business Achiever's Award, considered to be a benchmark for the new breed of dynamic entrepreneurs, who had made a mark in their respective fields, and made a difference through innovative approach and vision. I am the only publisher till date to be nominated in an impressive list of entrepreneurs and corporate leaders.

In 1998 my company, Comdex Computer Publishing, earned the pride of place in a leading computer trade journal, *Dataquest* that featured it as one of the sizzling IT companies in India. Incidentally mine was the only publishing company ever to be accorded this honour.

Given my new publishing concepts and innovative approach media generally keeps track of developments in my company. Mainline business magazines and dailies like *Business India*,

Business Today, *Economic Times*, and *Dataquest* often seek my views on publishing matters, and give extensive coverage to my books and publishing plans.

What are your views on globalisation and the role of MNCs publishing in India?

There is no denying the fact that globalisation has proven to be an engine of progress and prosperity and improving the quality of life for society at large. I feel its impact on improving the quality of Indian publishing has gone a long way. Today, almost all the major international publishers are operating in India with full-fledged publishing operations. Their contribution has been extremely positive, as they have been able to bring in the latest research and content in different fields and made that available to the Indian masses at the prices they can afford.

Further, I would like to add that books are the only commodity that is cheaper in India as compared to the rest of the world (one-tenth of the US prices). All the other commodities are either at the same price level or at higher prices in India than in other countries.

I feel multinational companies are contributing to the intellectual wealth of the country by publishing latest research and content on various subjects and making this available to the students of the developing world at an affordable price.

Do you find time to read? If so, on what subjects?

Being in the publishing business, I am fortunate to have access to all kinds of reading material and books. Despite having a busy work schedule, I always try to squeeze in some reading on a regular basis. My reading interests vary from technical subjects to financial, fiction and biographies of successful people—as these keep me well-informed and up to date with the current thought.

Do you enjoy travelling?

My job is such that it entails frequent travel all through the year—both domestic and international. Of course, I enjoy it quite a bit, as it allows me to meet new people and get exposure to a variety of experiences, besides time for reading.

Where do you see WILEY India five years from now?

I am quite sure that Wiley India would remain in a leadership position in publishing in India as it continues to bring world-class content to India, and delivers it at affordable prices. We also have major ambitious plans to further develop on our current online content delivery systems. Making new forays in different fields Wiley India also plans to become a global publishing centre of excellence for the parent company.

How is WILEY India meeting its corporate social responsibility?

In order to benefit the society at large and people from all walks of life Wiley makes the books available at one-tenth of their original US price. It has been our constant practice, and our way to contribute to the social good. We are also publishing Indian content for the world market enhancing the image of India and Indian authors.

How would you describe a good book?

The definition of a good book would vary depending upon its subject. In my opinion there are three types of books: Trade and fictions books, Academic textbooks and Reference books.

1. A good trade/fiction book should be able to engage the reader and make him feel as if he is really living that specific experience.
2. A good academic book is one which helps the student to learn in plain simple English without being burdened by the technical jargon.
3. A good reference book should bring the reader views from different experts on the same subject, with a proper index for easy reference.

So, different categories have different norms of being a good book.

Which role do you enjoy the most - entrepreneur, author, publisher or MD of the publishing company?

In fact, being the Managing Director of a publishing company affords me the experience of all these roles. In this position, I am able to contribute in different ways by offering my inputs in the business development as an entrepreneur, and giving an author's perspective in publishing and content development.

(Publishing Today, December 2009-January 2010)

VIKAS RAKHEJA
Publisher
Manjul Prakashan and Amaryllis

Transparency and integrity helps in building a brand

You belong to the 'Books' family, so to say. Please give us your background and tell us when and how you joined the book-trade?

You are right about me, belonging to the 'Books' family! My father, late Krishna Chandra Rakheja started Lyall Book Depot in Bhopal in 1956, in partnership with Sunder Dasji of Lyall Book Depot, Ludhiana. During my childhood and school days, I spent a lot of time at the bookshop, and subconsciously imbibed the love for books, I guess. In 1983, when I was in my first year of college, I started attending the bookshop on a regular basis, and started taking a keen interest in the purchase and sale of books at the shop. In the process, I met lots of different people, and learnt about various facets of the book trade. It fascinated me and I started liking it. The advantage that I had was that I had joined a well established bookstore, which was counted amongst the top 25 bookstores in the country. We dealt with Indian and foreign books in all subjects. Books were directly imported from abroad by the bookstore since early 50s and 60s! I lost my father in 1999, and subsequently, my mother in 2001.

When did you start Manjul Publishing House, and how did you think of publishing international bestsellers in Indian languages. What was the motivation behind it?

Manjul Publishing House was started in 1999. Manjul was my mother's name, and I decided to name the publishing house after her, as a mark of respect to her. A very large section of the Indian readership does not get to read a large body of excellent English writing in various genres, because they are not familiar with the English language. I had a dream to make international bestsellers accessible to the Indian readers in their own language. This motivated me to start publishing quality books in Hindi as well.

The first title to come out under Manjul was *Garbhavastha*, the Hindi translation of *Pregnancy* by Nutan Pandit. Then there was the Hindi edition of Sanjeev Kapoor's *Khazana of Indian Recipes*, which was his first book. This was followed by *Who Moved My Cheese* by Spencer Johnson. What seemed to be impossible in the beginning not only became possible, but also took off with flying colours. This was because of our commitment and vision, and largely through the unstinting support and encouragement of our readers. It was a common assumption at that time that regional Indian readers do not buy books and that language books do not have much of a market in India. We succeeded in shattering this myth, breaking new grounds by successfully publishing quality books in Hindi, as well as in Bangla, Marathi, Telugu, Tamil, Gujarati, Malayalam and Punjabi. Initially, we did face some ridicule from our peers in the publishing industry. But now that we have successfully created a niche for Indian language translations, even bigwigs like Penguin India and HarperCollins have joined the bandwagon by starting Hindi imprints of their own.

I have learnt that you are starting an English imprint, Amaryllis. Can you tell me more about it?

Yes, that's correct. We have just launched a new English imprint–Amaryllis which will publish the best in English fiction and non-fiction writing from India and across the world. Amaryllis will be based in New Delhi. We released our maiden catalogue of forthcoming authors on 2nd July, at the Taj Mahal Hotel, at the hands of Kapil Sibal, Minister of HRD where we also presented our authors to the media.

What are the activities you plan to handle from Delhi?

We have our Hindi pre-press set up in Bhopal, and print most of our books in Delhi at the Thomson Press. Our English editorial department for Amaryllis is based in Delhi, and so Amaryllis will be handled out of Delhi.

How do you distribute your books?

In October 2009, we formed a new distribution company S V Book Supply Company Pvt. Ltd., in association with Hind Pocket Books Pvt. Ltd. This is based in New Delhi, and has more than 1200 bookseller accounts throughout India, making books available in every nook and corner of the country. Our books are available at railway stations, airports, bus stands and all major bookshops across the country.

Which Manjul title has been an all-time bestseller?

The title *Jeevan Ek Khoj* by T. C. Chabbra, which is priced at Rs 60, has sold more than ten lakh copies in 2 years, in 4 languages

How did you acquire the Hindi rights for the Harry Potter series?

After noting the tremendous success of the Harry Potter series in English, we approached the agents for J K Rowlings – Christopher Little Literary Agency in London for the Indian language rights. We were told that there was to be a bidding amongst the ten interested parties. We bid an amount for Rs.10 lakhs as an advance against royalties, and to our delight, it was accepted without a hitch.

Which are the other International authors you have published?

We are proud to have published eminent names such as Rhonda Byrne, Stephan R Covey, Allan and Barbara Pease, Robert T Kiyosaki, John Templeton, John Gray, Dr Spencer Johnson, Zig Ziglar, Og Mandino, Dale Carnegie and Deepak Chopra, M Scott Peck, amongst others.

What makes a bestseller?

There are five basic things which makes a bestseller 1. The title, 2. The translation quality, 3. Pricing, 4. Production, and 5. Distribution. If one can manage these aspects expertly, a bestseller can be achieved. We have always paid utmost attention to all these five factors. This is why our books have successfully established the Manjul brand. Now, people come to the bookshops and ask for titles by Manjul.

What do you think makes Manjul a brand to reckon with?

I believe it's our transparency and integrity in dealing with authors, foreign publishers and literary agencies, and the blessings of people have helped us in establishing Manjul as a brand.

I understand that you are going to have some arrangement with Random House India, for publishing Hindi editions of their titles. Can you throw more light on this?

Random House India and we are in talks regarding an exclusive co-publishing agreement for Hindi editions of Random House popular titles. This will come through soon, and is a big achievement for us.

What do you think has been the impact of globalisation on Indian publishing?

Globalisation has proved to be good for the Indian publishing industry for authors, readers and publishers alike. Authors are now able to get very decent advances against royalty, and for publishers a large untapped market has become available. Readers of course have got a wider choice of subjects and authors to read.

Do you plan to get into e-publishing eventually?

Yes, e-publishing is the next big thing in publishing. We already have entered in this realm, in a way. One has to change with the times. E-publishing is here to stay and it is only a matter of time before it becomes a phenomenon.

Do you find time to read and what do you like to read?

I used to read a lot in the past. I read *The Fountain Head* by Ayn Rand, when I was in High School. I still take time out to go through popular books and magazines, apart from reviewing manuscripts.

Do other family members help you in your business?

I have two young sons. They are in class 9 and 10. My wife looks after the editorial division at our Bhopal office. She goes through each manuscript to check the quality of translation and gauge its readability. All book and cover designs are also done under her supervision.

(Publishing Today, June-July 2010)

Index

Abdulla, A, 48
Academic India Publishers, 6
Afro-Asian Countries Series, 83
Agarwal, Usha, 103
Agarwal, S C, 101–103. see also Sultan Chand & Sons
Ahuja, Kamal, 67–72
    daily routine, 72
    early career, 68
    export, 69
    future plans, 71
    globalisation's impact on marketing, 70–71
    good book, description of, 72
    marketing of books, 68
    marketing strategy, 70
    number of titles in a year, 70
    role model, 71
    selection process for recruitment, 69
    title selection, 70
    working methodology, 69
    see also Impulse Marketing
Akhil Bharatiya Hindi Prakashak Sangh, 11
Albert, Leo, 17–18
Ali, Mushtaq, 86
Al-Risala, 112. see also Khan, Saniyasnain
Amaryllis, see Rakheja, Vikas
Angel Publishing House, 6
Archer, Sir Jeffrey, 50
Arora, M G, 73–80
    Distinguished Booksellers Award (1997), 78
    distribution of work among family, 78
    early life, 74
    Excellence in Law Publishing Award (1998), 78
    experience in Tihar Jail during Emergency, 77
    good book, description of, 78
    hobbies, 80
    Lifetime Achievement Award (2008), 78
    Outstanding Contribution to the Book Trade (1999), 78
    place in Limca Book of Records, 78
    President of DSBPA, 77
    relations with multinationals, 79
    RSS membership, 74–75
    as a salesman and as a bookseller, 75
Arvind Kumar Publisher, see Kumar, Arvind
Atmaram & Sons, 62

Balan, Sridhar, 129–135
    Course Director, 131
    first regular job, 130
    freelance columnist, 130
    future of a book, 135
    good book, description of, 134
    hobbies, 133
    views on globalisation in publishing, 132
Bangalore Book Festival, 26
Bangalore Publishers and Booksellers Association, 26
Bar Association of India, 78
Basu, Durga Das, 17
Beri, Rajiv, 90–95

acquisition of Frank Brothers, 92
acquisition of typesetting companies, Charon Tec and ICC., 93
Capexil award, 91
cleared the IAS, 92
Corporate Social Responsibility, 95
electronic publishing, 94
focus areas of Macmillan, 94
globalisation impact on Indian publishing, 94
good book, description of, 95
job in Tata Mc-Graw Hill, 92
market share of Macmillan, 92
on-line publishing, 93
presentation to avoid piracy, 94
role as a Director, 95
turning points in Macmillan India, 93
Bhagat, Chetan, 87. see also Mehra, R K
Bhatt, Devru, 26
Bloomsbury, 35–36
Booksellers Association of India, 5, 18
BookStore, 93. see also Beri, Rajiv
A Brief History of Time, 115

CAPEXIL, 4, 21, 105, 138, 144
CAPEXIL, role of, 4
Central Law Agency, 75. see also Arora, M G
Chandrasekar, S, 48
Chawla, C M, 137, 139
Chennai Book Fair (CBF), 48–49
Chicken Soup Series, 143. see also Mehta, Sunil
Children's Book Fair, 83
Choudhury, Kanti, 11
Chowdhury Export House, 1–8. see also Chowdhury, A S
Chowdhury, A S, 1–8
  awards, 5–6
  Career Events – Passport for Success (magazine), 3
  disciplined life, 2
  early age struggle, 2
  Election Officer of FPBA, 5
  export of books to Thailand, 3
  export of books, problems, 4
  life style, 2
  life's aim, 3
  principles of happy and healthy life, 7–8
  see also Goodwill Books International; Chowdhury Export House
Chowdhury, Amber Raj (son of A S Chowdhury), 6
Chowdhury, Rajneesh (son of A S Chowdhury), 6
Comdex, 155
Cracking the Code, 155
cross-cultural marriages, 12

Dalai Lama, 20
Das, Jatin, 57
Das, Sukumar, 136–140
  chairman, books panel of CAPEXIL, 138
  digital printing, 139
  future plans for UBS, 139
  good book, description of, 140
  impact of globalisation on Indian Publishing, 139
  joining at UBS, 137
  online business, 139
  president, FPBAI, 138
  relationship with Chawlas, 139
  secretary general, Afro Asian Book Council, 138
  success mantra for young entrepreneurs, 139–140
Delhi Book Fair, 18–19
Delhi Shops and Establishment Act, 76
Delhi State Booksellers and Publishers Association, 5
Delivery of Books Act, 50
Desai, Anita, 36–37
Deshpande, Shyam, 123–128
  from teaching to publishing, 124
  Globalisation's effect on publishing, 127

nature of Marathi publishing, views, 127
special project, 126
Devidayal, Namita, 36
Dhara (daughter of Shyam Deshpande), 128
Dharmarajan, Geeta, 54–60
   daily life, 60
   Founder and Executive Director, Katha, 54
   future plans, 60
   globalisation's impact on publishing, 59–60
   good book, description of, 60
   Katha InfoTech and eCom School, 58
   Katha Prize Stories, 57
   Katha Reading Campaign, 58
   Katha's storybooks, 58
   social responsibility, 59
   STORY telling, 56
   Tamasha! children's story magazine, 55
   unknown authors books, 57
   well-known artist's contribution for covers, 57
digital media, 44
digital publishing, 20, 38, 94, 99, 120
Dreamtech Press Pvt Ltd., 154. *see also* Gupta, Vikas
Duggal, K S, 11

e-books, 21, 64
Ettinger, Richard Prentice, 18

Farewell to Cricket, 86. *see also* Mehra, R K
Federation of Educational Publishers, 5
Federation of Indian Publishers, 5, 18, 27
Five Point Someone, 87. *see also* Mehra, R K
Foreign Publishers, entry into India, 20–21
Frankfurt Book Fair, 13, 31, 82

Gangaram Book Bureau, 26
Gangaram, N, 26
Gaurav (son of S K Ghai), 109
Ghai, O P, 18, 20, 105, 107
Ghai, S K, 104–110
   e-journal *Publishing Today*, 108
   future plans, 108
   globalisation's impact on publishing, 109
   good book, description of, 107
   participation in book fairs, 106
   piracy and copyright violations, views on, 109
   PL-480 program, 106
   Sterling Publishers, incorporation of, 105–106
   subsidiary rights, 106
   visualisation about industry, 110
Ghosh, Asoke K., 16–23
   Chairman of CAPEXIL Books Panel, 21
   Chairman of Indian Reprographic Rights Organisation (IRRO), 19
   Chairman of the Delhi Book Fair, 18-19
   Federation of Indian Publishers, founder member, 18
   Printing Technology and Graphic Arts course, 17
   social responsibility, 22
   STM books, 21
   tie-ups with international publishers, 23
   Times of India, joining in, 17
Go Raksha Andolan, 77
Good Offices Committee (GOC), 77
Goodwill Books International, *see* Chowdhury, A S
Goodwill Publishing House, 6
Goodword Books (Pvt.) Ltd., *see* Khan, Saniyasnain
Goodword Kidz, 113. *see also* Khan, Saniyasnain
A Guide to Pathology (1969), 63. *see also* Vij, J P
Gujarati, B S, 106
Gumaste, V H, 150

Gupta, Vikas, 153–158
  Comdex, 155
  corporate social responsibility, 157
  Cracking the Code, 155
  good book, description of, 157
  Rapidex, 155
  role of MNCs publishing, 156
  Sista World Com Young Business Achiever's Award (1998), 155
  views on globalisation, 156
  WILEY's future prospects, 157

Hanif, Mohammed, 36
HarperCollins India, 42
Hassan, Nuzhat, 81–84
  Book Club scheme, 84
  good book, description of, 84
  hobbies, 84
  major thrust areas of NBT, 84
  mobile vans of NBT, 84
  NBT Book Club, 83
Hind Pocket Books Pvt. Ltd., 162. see also Rakheja, Vikas

Idols, 86. see also Mehra, R K
Impulse Marketing, see Ahuja, Kamal
India Book House, 26
Indian Diaspora Studies, 83
Indian National Trust for Art, Culture and Heritage (INTACH), 55
Indian Publishing since Independence, 108
Indian Reprographic Rights Organisation (IRRO), 19
Institute of Book Publishing, 104, 107. see also Ghai, S K
International Alliance of Independent Publishers, 100. see also Menon, Ritu
International Forum for Reproduction Rights Organisations (IFRRO), 19
International Publishers Association (IPA), 18
International Rights Exhibition of the Works, 82

ISBN and barcoding, 50, 145

Jai Prakash Narain, 77
Jain, Dhanesh, 40–44
  Academic Division for Libraries, 42
  business growth, 43
  buzz word, 42
  dictionary division, 42
  early stage of publishing, 41
  good book, description of, 43
  marketing network, 42
  mission statement, 42
  MNC's role in publishing, 44
  teaching at JNU, 41
Jain, Sugat, (son of Dhanesh Jain), 43
Jaypee Brothers Medical Publishers, see Vij, J P
Jaypee Medical International, see Vij, J P
Jaypee Pharma Customised Imprints, see Vij, J P
Jeevan Ek Khoj, 162. see also Rakheja, Vikas

Kali for Women, 98
Kannadhasan, Gandhi, 45–53
  Chennai Book Fair, 48–49
  controversy regarding the copyright of father's work, 52–53
  export of Tamil books, 51
  globalisation impact on Tamil publishing, 50
  good book, description of, 52
  ISBN and barcoding, 50
  online selling, 51
  overseas branches, 46–47
  policy on vanity publishing, 49–50
  President of Booksellers and Publishers Association of South India (BAPASI), 47
  shopping mall culture, 50
  social responsibility, 51
Kannadhasan, Pathippagam, 45. see also Kannadhasan, Gandhi

Kannadhasan, Murali (son of Gandhi Kannadhasan), 51
Kapish (son of R K Mehra), 89
Karthika, V K, 119
Karunatilaka, Shehan, 36
Katha, 54. see also Dharmarajan, Geeta
Khan, Maulana Wahiduddin (father of Saniyasnain Khan), 112
Khan, Saniyasnain, 111–115
   attraction for publishing, 112
   children's books, 113
   good book, description of, 115
   Islamic books, 112
   marketing of books, 113
   mission of, 113
   participation in international fairs, 114
   price-sensitive markets, 113
Khanam, Farida (sister of Saniyasnain Khan), 114
Kiran Publications, 3
Krishnamurti, K, 48
Kumar, Arvind, 9–15
   auto engineering, 10
   family life, 12
   first Director of NBT, 12
   future plans, 14
   Gandhian principle of self-denial, 12
   good book, description of, 15
   model of school book clubs, 10
   reading habits, perceptions, 15
   relations with well-known authors, 14
   Scholastic job, 10
   Scholastic, job in, 13
   school book fairs, 10
Kumar, H L, 76
Kumar, Narendra, 108
Kumar, Ulhas, 26

Library of Congress Office, 11
Life and Times of Ismat Chughtai, 57

Macmillan India Ltd., see Beri, Rajiv
Mahatma Gandhi, 82
Malhotra, D N, 18, 20, 108
Manjul Prakashan, see Rakheja, Vikas
Mankad, Vinoo, 86
Mapin Publishing (Pvt.) Ltd., see Shah, Bipin
MapinLit, 30. see also Shah, Bipin
Marathi Prakashak Sangh, 146
Marathi publishing, 124. see also Deshpande, Shyam
Mathur, Anurag, 87. see also Mehra, R K
Matthew, K V, 48
Mehra, D (grand uncle of R K Mehra), 86
Mehra, N D, (father of R K Mehra), 86
Mehra, R K, 85–89
   e-publishing, 88
   follower of cricket, 86
   future plans, 89
   good book, description of, 89
   logo of Rupa & Co, 88
   marketing network, 88
   pillar of Indian trade publishing, 88
   responsibilities of, 87
   sale of subsidiary rights, 88
   workforce of Rupa & Co, 87
Mehta Publishing House, see Mehta, Sunil
Mehta, Anil (father of Sunil Mehta), 142
Mehta, Sunil, 141–147
   children's books in four colour, 144
   good book, description of, 146–147
   impact of globalisation on Marathi language publishing, 146
   ISBN and barcoding, 145
   Man Booker Prize (2000), 143
   Mehta Marathi Granth Jagat magazine, 144–145
   online selling, 144
   pioneer in publishing bestsellers in Marathi, 143
   shopping mall culture, 146

T Book Club, concept, 145
  unfriendly stand of selling books on cash basis, 142
Mehta, Tyeb, 57
Menon, Anjolie Ela, 57
Menon, Ritu, 96–100
  break up with Urvashi Butalia, 98
  digital publishing, views on, 99
  globalisation in publishing, views on, 99
  good book, description of, 99
  manuscript selection, criteria, 98
  marketing of books, 100
  marketing subsidiary rights, 99
  Orient Longman, joining in, 97
  Vikas Publishing House, joining in, 97
Mergers and acquisitions, 43, 65
Modi, K K, 150
Mueenuddin, Daniyal, 36
Mukherje, Saugata, 116–122
  digital publishing, onset of, 120–121
  experience at Harper Collins, 117
  experiences at A M Heath & Co., 118
  globalisation's impact on publishing, 120
  good book, description of, 120
  Harper Collins (HC), joined as copy editor, 117
  hobbies of, 121
  Jerusalem International Fellowship Programme (2007), 121
  memorable catch at Rupa, 118
  Paul Hamlyn fellowship, 121
  royalties, views on, 121
  social responsibility, 122
  views on the copyright amendments, 121
Mukherjee, Sujit, 97

Nair, K P R, 131
Naraynan, K R, 76
National Book Development Council, 11. *see also* Kumar, Arvind
National Book Policy, 11. *see also* Kumar, Arivnd
National Book Trust
  Afro-Asian Countries Series, 83
  Book Club Scheme, 83
  Golden Jubilee celebrations of, 84
  Indian Diaspora Studies, 83
  major thrust areas of, 84
  mobile vans, 84
  Popular Social Science, 83
  see also Hassan, Nuzhat
Nationalisation of Textbooks, 44
Nayantara Sahgal's biography, *see* Menon, Ritu
NCBA Exports (Pvt.) Ltd., 136. *see also* Das, Sukumar
Nesfield Grammar, 93. *see also* Beri, Rajiv
Net Book Agreement (NBA), 151. *see also* Shanbhag, Tekatte Narayan
New Delhi World Book Fair (NDWBF), 82
One Night @ the Call Center, 87. *see also* Mehra, R K
One to One: Glimpses of Indian Publishing Industry, 108. *see also* Ghai, S K
online promotion, 22

Padma Shri Award recipient, *see* Menon, Ritu; Shanbhag, Tekatte Narayan,
Padmanabhan, A, 48
Pan Macmillan and Picador India, *see* Mukherje, Saugata
Pattanayak, D P, 11
Peer, Basharat, 36
Penguin India Books, 34. *see also* Sarkar, Chiki
PHI Learning (Pvt.) Ltd., 16–23. *see also* Ghosh, Asoke. K.
Popular Social Science, 83
Prasanna, E, 86
Pratima (wife of Shyam Deshpande), 128
Printed verses digital book, royalties, 38, 121

Radhakrishna Prakashan, 11. *see also* Kumar, Arvind
Rajhans Publications, 123. *see also* Deshpande, Shyam
Rakheja, Krishna Chandra (father of Vikas Rakheja), 160
Rakheja, Vikas, 159–164
  Amaryllis (an English imprint), 161
  bestseller, description of, 163
  books distribution, 162
  e-publishing, views on, 163
  first title, 161
  Hindi rights for the Harry Potter series, 162
  international authors, 162
  pre-press set up, 162
  views on impact of globalisation on Indian publishing, 163
Rao, Raja Rameshwar, 97
Rapidex, 155
Ratna Sagar (Pvt.) Ltd., 40–44. *see also* Balan, Sridhar
Ray, Satyajit, 88
reading habits, 15, 58, 102
Right to Property and Fundamental Rights, 130. *see also* Balan, Sridhar
Rimjhim Ghosh Foundation, 22. *see also* Ghosh, Asoke K
Robinson, D R, 13
Rupa & Co., 85–89. *see also* Mehra, R K
Rushdie, Salman, 20, 37
Russian literature, 83

S V Book Supply Company, 162. *see also* Rakheja, Vikas
Sakoian, Carol, 13
Samayik Sahitya journal 11. *see also* Kumar, Arvind
Sampoorna Kranti Movement, 77
Sarabhai, Sir Ambalal, 150
Sarabhai, Mallika. *see also* Shah, Bipin, 32–33
Sarkar, Chiki, 34–39
  acquisition in fiction and non-fiction, 36
  Editor-Publisher, Penguin India Books, 34
  education, 35
  first job, 35
  good book, description of, 38
  hobbies, 39
  Random House, job in, 35
  social responsibility, views, 39
  views on the copyright amendments, 39
Sarva Shiksha Abhiyan (SSA), 145
Satish Agencies, 26
Scholastic India, 10. *see also* Arvind Kumar
Sethi, Aman, 36
Sethi, S C, 102
Shah, Bipin, 29–33
  art publisher, 30
  co-publishing with international publishers and museums, 32
  Doubleday's international division, 30
  impact of globalisation, 32
  marketing of books, 31
  participation and experience in international book fairs, 31–32
  reading interests, 33
  relations with international publishers and museums, 31
Shanbhag, Tekatte Narayan, 148–152
  illustrious list of clients, 151
  legendary bookseller, 149
  literary influence, 151
  Padma Shri (2003) award recipient, 149, 152
Sharma, Shankar Dayal, 20
Shastri, Lal Bahadur, 75–76, 106
shopping malls, 27, 110
Sidhwani, Balram, 24–28
  Bangalore Publishers and Booksellers Association, 26
  Director, UBS Publishers Distributors, 24
  own bookshops, 28
  views on ebooks, 27
Sobers, Gary, 86

Sobti, Krishna, 14
Sterling Paperbacks (1972), 106. see also Ghai, S K
Sterling Publishers (P) Ltd., 104. see also Ghai, S K
STM books, 17, 21
Strand Bookstall, see Shanbhag, Tekatte Narayan
Subramanian, N A V, 48
Subrhamanyam, N, 131
Sukumar, P M, 119
Sultan Chand & Sons, 101. see also Agarwal, S C
Sri Sultan Chand Dropadi Devi Education Foundation, 103
Shri Sultan Chand Trust (1990), 103
Sultan Chandji, 102
Sundaram, K P, 25
Sunny Days, 86. see also Mehra, R K
Swami, Shrimanyogi (Shivaji's Biography), 143. see also Mehta, Sunil

Tagore, Rabindranath, 93
Tamasha! (children's story magazine), 55
Tamil publisher, see Kannadhasan, Gandhi
Textbook prescription, 11
Thairani, Kala, 11
The 3 Mistakes of my Life, 87. see also Mehra, R K
The Book Industry in India: Context, Challenge and Strategy, 138. see also Das, Sukumar

UBS Publishers Distributors, 24, 136. see also Das, Sukumar; Sidhwani, Balram
UK bestseller vs. Indian bestseller, 37
Ultrasound in Obstetrics and Gynecology, 64. see also Vij, J P
Universal Book Traders, see Arora, M G
Universal Law Publishing Company, see Arora, M G

University Publishers, 105. see also Ghai, S K
Dr Usha Agarwal Trust (2004), 103

Vahitale Balpan (Childhood in a Notebook), 124. see also Deshpande, Shyam
Venu, Satish, 26
Verma, Dev Raj, 3
Vij and Rama Publishing House, 62. see also Vij, J P
Vij, J P, 61–66
  acquisitions and mergers, 65
  advance royalty, 64
  areas of operations, 63
  competition in medical publishing, 65
  cricket match between Indian and foreign publishers, 66
  domestic sales, 64
  e-medical books, 64
  good book description of, 66
  leading medical publishers in Asia, 62
  marketing efforts, 65
  medical journals, 64
  new developments, 65
  selling rights, 64
  target readers, 63
Vij, Raman (wife of J P Vij), 66
Vij, Sohan Lal (father of J P Vij), 62
Vikas (son of S K Ghai), 109
von Holtzbrinck, Stefan, 120

Wiley India (Pvt.) Ltd., see Gupta, Vikas
Women Unlimited, see Menon, Ritu
World Literacy Day, 56

Young Learner Publications, 6

Zaidi, Atiya, 43
Zed Books, 97
Zutshi, Ashok, 41

Contacts

A.S.Choudhury: goodwillbooksinternational@gmail.com
Arvind Kumar: arvindkr@sify.com
Asoke K Ghosh: asokeghosh@phindia.com
Balram Sidhwani: balram@bngm.ubspd.com
Bipin Shah: mapin@mapinpub.com
Chiki Sarkar: chiki.sarkar@gmail.com
Dhanesh Jain: rsagar@ratnasagar.com
Gandhi Kannadhasan: gandhikannadasan@gmail.com
Geeta Dharmarajan: geeta@katha.org
J.P.Vij: jpvij.cmd@gmail.com ; jaypee@jaypeebrothers.com
Kamal Ahuja: adarshpublications@gmail.com
M.G.Arora: unilaw@vsnl.com
Nuzhat Hassan: nuzhathassan@gmail.com
R.K.Mehra: rupa@ndb.vsnl.net.in
Rajiv Beri: rajivberi10@gmail.com
Ritu Menon: womenunltd@vsnl.net
S.C.Aggarwal: ypsabharwal@yahoo.com
S.K.Ghai: skg@sterlingpublishers.com
Saniyasnain Khan: info@goodwordbooks.com
Saugata Mukherjee: saugata.mukherjee@gmail.com
Shyam Deshpande,
    Rajhans Prakashan, Shivalik Apartment, Samadhan Colony,
    Aurangpura, B/H Dist Colony, Aurangabad-431005
Sridhar Balan: sridbalan@gmail.com
Sukumar Das: sukumar4das21@gmail.com
Sunil Mehta: mehpubl@vsnl.com
Tekkatte Narayan Shanbhag: info@strandbookstall.com
Vikas Gupta: vgupta@wiley.com
Vikas Rakheja: vikas@manjulindia.com

Institute of Book Publishing

The importance of books in the intellectual, cultural and educational development of a country has long been recognised. But it is only in recent years that book publishing has acquired its rightful place as an industry.

Responding to the growing need for professionally-trained and well-honed personnel to feed this growing industry, the Institute of Book Publishing was founded in 1985 at the initiative of the Late Shri O P Ghai, who was not only a pioneer in Indian book publishing, but also a visionary who could understand the significance of specialised training and research in the various aspects of book publishing.

The institute runs an annual Condensed Course for publishing professionals since 1986. Apart from getting participants from all over India, it also gets participants regularly from neighbouring countries, South Asia and Southeast Asia, Africa and now from Europe as well. The 25th Condensed Course for Publishing Professionals will be held from Nov. 19-28, 2012.

It organises short-term courses and specialised courses from time to time. It has also developed Intensive Course for Editors in Book Publishing, the fifth course will be held in Delhi from 21-26, May, 2012. The Institute's Courses are run without any governmental or institutional aid.

The Institute faculty includes academicians, professionals and directors of major publishing houses in India. The Institute's alumni hold senior positions in their organisations and we are in the process of forming alumni association of the Institute at the 20th New Delhi World Book Fair.

It has also developed a library containing books on books and various aspects of publishing industry. It publishes *Publishing Today* an e-journal since December 2006.